THE STALKER

Other Scholastic titles
you will enjoy:

The Body
by Carol Ellis

Spring Break
by Barbara Steiner

Night School
by Caroline B. Cooney

The Train
by Diane Hoh

THE STALKER

CAROL ELLIS

SCHOLASTIC INC.
New York Toronto London Auckland Sydney

No part of this publication may be reproduced in whole or in part, or stored in a retrieval system, or transmitted in any form or by any means, electronic, mechanical, photocopying, recording, or otherwise, without written permission of the publisher. For information regarding permission, write to Scholastic Inc., 555 Broadway, New York, NY 10012.

ISBN 0-590-25520-7

12 11 10 9 8 7 6 5 4 3 2 1   6 7 8 9/9 0 1/0

Printed in the U.S.A.   01

First Scholastic printing, January 1996

Prologue
Opening Night

The theater was dark now.

Only the green glow of the exit signs and a dim bulb in the wings gave off any light.

As eighteen-year-old Janna Richards crossed the stage toward a side exit, she suddenly stopped. Center stage now, she turned and faced the empty seats.

In her mind's eye, Janna saw the audience that had been there earlier that night. Their eyes focused on the stage. Their lips curved in smiles. Eager. Expectant. Ready to be entertained.

She heard the laughter again. The hush during a quiet scene. The applause. Wave after wave of it, like a thundering waterfall.

Janna couldn't resist. Imagining the applause and the cheers, she took a bow. Blew a couple of kisses and bowed again.

As she straightened up, grinning at herself, a bright hot glare hit her in the eyes.

Shading her eyes, Janna peered up at the catwalk, a narrow metal walkway suspended from the auditorium ceiling. All she could make out was the outline of a figure, crouched low behind one of the lights.

"Okay, you caught me," she called out, laughing. "Go ahead, make fun. Tell the director how I was pretending to be the star, I don't care."

No answer.

Janna shrugged and started to leave.

The spotlight followed her movement.

She stopped, peering up at the light.

"Okay, who is that?" she called.

Still no answer.

"Come on, who is it?" Janna demanded. "Is this some kind of joke?"

Janna's scalp prickled.

Tightening her grip on her dance bag, she began walking offstage.

Again, the spotlight followed her.

"This is a weird game you're playing, whoever you are!" Janna shouted, picking up her pace.

She was almost offstage when she heard the catwalk creak. Nervously, she looked up.

The crouched figure was standing now. Janna saw a flash of skin. And then something was sailing through the air, coming directly at her. Before Janna could move, it had landed in the pool of light at her feet.

A single red rose.

A card tied to the stem with white satin ribbon.

A message that said, *Soon you'll be mine, Janna.*

Chapter 1

As the auditorium shook to the sound of a fifties rock-and-roll beat, Janna and her partner, Eric Fischer, moved to center stage. Eric spun Janna around three times, pulled her to him, then spun her back out again.

"Doo-wop da-dooby-do," the entire cast, twenty-one strong, sang as they danced the L.A. Hustle.

The musical was *Grease*.

The set was the "Burger Palace," complete with booths, soda fountain, and jukebox. The cast, guys in black leather jackets and ducktails, girls with teased hair and bobby socks, were from the Regional Theater Company.

It was the third night and the house was packed again. Third night on a tour that would take the show all over two midwestern states.

And you're part of it, Janna told herself.

You're actually dancing with a professional theater company.

Janna had fallen in love with dancing and the theater when she was six and saw a performance of *The Nutcracker*. She'd gone home, stood in front of a mirror, and danced. The Sugar Plum Fairy, of course.

After that came lessons. Ballet, tap, modern. The work was hard, but Janna was determined to dance professionally someday. Her parents were hardly rich, and as soon as she was old enough to work part-time jobs, she helped pay for the lessons. She jumped at the chance to audition for every school play and local theater production and usually got a part. Being able to sing was a plus.

So were her looks. Long, thick hair, almost black. Big, snapping brown eyes in a heart-shaped face. A wide mouth and a smile that reached to the back row of the theater. And a dancer's graceful, muscular body.

"We'll always be together!" The cast sang the final words to the song. Janna and Eric, still prominent, ended their routine with Janna doing a split in front of her partner with her arms raised above her head.

The audience erupted in applause. Janna held her pose until the red velvet curtain billowed shut, then she leaped up and rushed offstage.

Controlled chaos. The entire company scurried around in the wings, getting into position for curtain calls. Gray Williams, the choreographer, nodded at Janna as she passed by. He was a tall, slender man of about forty-five, with dark hair and an always serious expression in his piercing eyes.

"Nice work, Janna," he said.

"Thanks, Gray." Janna couldn't believe it. A compliment from Gray Williams was like rain in the desert.

Janna was listed in the program as a "dancer," and most of the time, she was in the background. But during rehearsals, Gray had given her and her partner a prominent role in the final number.

Since this was Janna's first professional job as a dancer, she'd never expected to be singled out. And she wasn't kidding herself — as far as fame went, she wasn't at the top, or even in the middle. But for about thirty seconds at the end of the show, she was actually in the spotlight.

"You've got nice energy. Good presence," Gray said. "Keep it up." He spoke casually, as if he were telling her the time.

Janna thanked him again. Cool and casual like he was. As if she didn't feel like hopping up and down and screaming from excitement.

Turning away from Gray, Janna bumped into Liz Thompson, another dancer and one of her roommates.

"I heard what Gray said," Liz told her. "Don't get too blissed out. The first mistake you make, he'll be all over you."

"Oh?"

Liz nodded, tucking a strand of icy blond hair into place. Icy. That was the word for Liz Thompson, Janna thought. The only place she warmed up was onstage.

"I just thought I'd let you know," Liz added. "He gave me a feature dance last summer. I was all of one second late on an entrance and he told me I'd ruined the entire production. He's a real perfectionist, in case you haven't noticed. So watch your step."

You had to have been more than a second late, Janna thought. It was probably more like a minute. But she didn't say it. She had to share rooms with the girl, after all.

And Liz *was* a good dancer. Janna knew Liz thought Gray should have given her that final number. Ever since he'd given it to Janna, Liz's iciness had turned arctic. Except when she was being snide and sarcastic, which was even worse.

But you're just as good a dancer, Janna told herself. You deserve that moment in the spotlight. You know she's jealous, so don't let her get to you. "Thanks for the warning, Liz," she said.

Moving away from Liz, Janna caught sight of Ryan Mitchell, the assistant stage manager. He was standing offstage, making sure everyone was in the right place.

That's Ryan, Janna thought. Always in the background, behind the scenes. Always with those intense, watchful eyes.

He'd caught Janna's attention the minute she'd seen him. Dark blond hair. Green eyes with gold flecks in them. A lean, almost bony face and a way of walking that reminded Janna of a cat on the prowl.

Very cute.

Also very quiet. Ryan kept to himself. Was he shy? A snob? Janna didn't know, but she wanted to find out.

As she rushed by him, she threw him one of her back-row smiles.

"Hey, Janna, got a sec?" Ryan reached out and put a hand on her arm.

Yess! Janna thought. He wants to talk. A definite step in the right direction.

"Sure," she said, wiping a trickle of sweat off her forehead.

Ryan held out an envelope with her name on it. "I found this on the floor outside your dressing room," he explained.

"Thanks." Okay, so he didn't want to talk. This wasn't a good time, anyway.

"Good show, by the way." Ryan squeezed her arm, then turned away as someone began complaining to him about a lost prop.

As Janna started to open the envelope, her dancing partner came running up. "Let's go, Richards," Eric said breathlessly. "Curtain's going up." He grabbed her hand and pulled her toward the stage.

The band played the finale, and the applause swelled again as the curtain swept open.

Janna stuffed the envelope inside the waistband of her plaid chiffon dress. When it was their turn, she and Eric ran onstage and joined the line of other chorus members.

Janna loved this part. The start of the show was more exciting — the anticipation, the butterflies in her stomach. But curtain calls were pure fun. The cast relaxed now, the audience smiling and clapping their approval.

Janna loved it. The applause for dancing her heart out. The approving smiles. The audience's eyes on her.

Straightening up from the first bow, Janna lifted her eyes toward the balcony. Crouched on the catwalk above the auditorium, one of the lighting crew swept the big follow spot back and forth across the stage.

The sight brought back the memory of opening night. Two nights before, when she'd stood alone onstage and seen someone crouched behind that same spotlight.

Unmoving.

Unspeaking.

Watching her.

Throwing her a rose. *Soon you'll be mine, Janna.*

Bowing a second time, Janna staggered slightly. Eric tightened his grip on her hand. "You okay, Richards?" he muttered out of the side of his mouth.

"Sure," she muttered back. "Just got dizzy for a second."

"Yeah," Eric said dryly. "Fame goes to your head, doesn't it?"

Janna kept her smile in place. But every

time the spotlight swept across her eyes, she flashed on that solitary figure.

Who was it? Who'd been watching her?

Four curtain calls later, the show was over.

The feeling backstage was different now. Still wired, but beginning to loosen. Beginning to feel tired and hungry — things they ignored during the performance.

As soon as she was offstage, Janna loosened the waistband on her dress and took a deep breath.

As she went downstairs to the dressing room she shared with three other dancers, she tore open the envelope Ryan had given her and pulled out a single sheet of paper.

Janna, it said in bright red ink, *hope you break a leg.*

Janna's stomach started churning. But not because of the words. After all, "break a leg" meant good luck in the theater.

But whoever had sent her this message wasn't wishing her luck.

Below the words was a drawing of a human leg. Crude, but clear.

It was a dancer's leg, kicking high, the toes pointed in a black ballet shoe.

But the leg had been chopped off just below

the knee. Shiny white bone stuck out from ragged flesh.

And blood spurted out like a fountain, covering the sheet of paper in glistening red drops.

Chapter 2

Jimmy, Janna thought with a shudder. Jimmy Dare.

Her ex-boyfriend.

An image of him appeared in Janna's mind. His face dark with anger. His eyes glowing like coals. "You'll be sorry about this, Janna," he'd said. "You'll wish you'd never taken this lousy job."

It was the last time they'd seen each other before Janna left on tour.

Jimmy Dare was a bright, good-looking guy. A great build. A cleft in his chin. He could be funny. Sometimes he could even be sweet — as long as he got his way.

But stand up to him and his dark eyes shot sparks. His soft, silky voice turned rough.

Janna knew. She'd stood up to him plenty of times during the eight months they'd dated.

Even before graduating from high school, Janna knew he was a mistake. Jimmy wanted to control her. Wanted her to jump when he snapped his fingers.

She'd been a coward, she admitted that now. They were going to different colleges, so she figured they'd just drift apart. There wouldn't be any need for a big break-up scene.

No such luck.

When he heard about her job with the theater company, he'd gone ballistic. "A musical? Traveling around two states?" he'd shouted. "When are we supposed to see each other, Janna? Tell me that!"

Never, Janna thought. What she'd said was, "Maybe you can make it to one of the shows. Glenwood Junction is only fifty miles from here."

"Sure," he said sarcastically. "That'll be great, Janna. You want me to drive fifty miles to Glenwood Junction, sit on my butt in a stuffy theater for two hours, and then *maybe* you'll spend half an hour with me?"

Janna's temper flared. "Gee, Jimmy, I'd sure hate for you to sit on your butt for two hours and watch me dance!" she shot back. "I mean, it's only the most important thing in my life.

But maybe the house'll be sold out and you can stand!"

They'd argued and shouted for an hour. And then Jimmy had stomped out. But first, he told her she'd be sorry.

And now this, Janna thought, looking at the horrible drawing.

She'd *never* be sorry about getting this job. It meant everything to her.

But she sure was sorry about ever getting mixed up with Jimmy Dare.

Janna remembered the figure in the empty theater again.

She could see Jimmy sneaking inside, spotting her staying late. Climbing up to the catwalk and scaring her with that light. That rose and its card.

Sweet, then nasty — that was definitely Jimmy's style.

And so was this drawing.

Furious and disgusted, Janna wadded the drawing and the envelope into a ball and tossed them into a trash barrel. Then she headed for the dressing room.

She'd handled Jimmy before.

If he was around now, she'd be ready for him.

* * *

"Finally!" Toni Gabriel cried, as Janna entered the steamy, crowded dressing room. Another dancer and roommate of Janna's, she was a bubbly, gray-eyed redhead with a breathy speaking voice that surprised everybody when she belted out a song. "You made a big hit with somebody, Janna. Look!"

Janna's eyes snapped to the dressing-room table — a long counter cluttered with tubes and jars of makeup, boxes of tissues, cups of water, and stray pieces of clothing.

At Janna's own space was a bouquet of roses, their red blooms poking out from flimsy green tissue paper.

Roses. Not just one this time. A whole bouquet.

"It's a good thing you came in just now." Gillian Waters, Janna's third roommate, wiped greasepaint off her forehead and smiled at Janna in the mirror. "I practically had to tie Toni down to keep her from reading the card."

"So go on, Janna!" Toni urged excitedly. "Tell us who they're from."

"Yeah," Liz Thompson said, her face smeared with thick white cold cream. "I won't be able to sleep unless I find out."

"Jealous, Liz?" Gillian asked, brushing out

her wavy brown hair. Gillian was usually serious and intense, but she enjoyed taking little jabs at Liz.

"Oh, insanely," Liz said. She tore a handful of tissues from a box and started wiping her face. "I'm definitely insanely jealous."

Ignoring Liz, Janna dug into the green paper and pulled out the small white envelope. The card inside said simply, *Soon, Janna.*

"Hey, what's wrong?" Toni asked. "You don't look exactly thrilled."

"I'm not," Janna said, handing her the card. "I love roses, but this is really kind of weird."

"*Soon, Janna.*" Toni frowned as she read the message aloud. "I don't — oh. They're from the same person, aren't they? The one who threw the rose at you opening night."

"Are you sure?" Gillian asked, frowning as she peered over Toni's shoulder at the card.

"The first one said, 'Soon you'll be mine,'" Janna reminded her. "This one leaves out a couple of words, but it says the same thing."

"Listen, Janna, keep your eyes open from now on," Gillian warned. "I mean, you've read about fans who get these obsessive crushes on famous people, right? They send flowers and cards, just like this. Some of them are totally harmless, but . . ."

"Come on, Janna's not exactly a celebrity," Liz interrupted, wiping the last traces of makeup from her face. "Don't start getting all dramatic, Gillian."

"I only get dramatic onstage, Liz," Gillian shot back. "Besides, how many normal people sneak into a theater and toss down roses from a catwalk?"

"Oh, please!" Liz rolled her eyes. "No one sneaked anywhere. Somebody from the lighting crew probably has a completely harmless crush on Janna. Or else he's playing a joke."

"Yeah, well, I'm not exactly hysterical with laughter," Janna said. She took the card from Toni and ripped it in half. "And I have a pretty good idea who's doing this."

"Who?" Toni asked, anxiously.

"Jimmy Dare. My *ex*-boyfriend." Janna dipped her fingers into a large jar of cold cream. "I've heard from him already, as a matter of fact."

As she described the drawing of the chopped-off leg, Toni's eyes widened. "Why would he send you something so disgusting and then give you roses?"

"Jimmy's like that," Janna explained with a sigh. "Really nice one day and totally horrible the next."

"Sounds like he enjoys playing mind games," Liz said, brushing out her hair.

You ought to know, Janna thought. Mind games were one of Liz's specialties.

As Janna cleaned her face and brushed her hair, her gaze kept falling on the roses. Their scent was overpowering in the steamy dressing room.

Sweet.

Almost sickening.

Soon you'll be mine.

Soon.

It felt more like a warning than a promise.

Half an hour later, when she and her three roommates left the theater, Janna took the bouquet of flowers with her.

"Look," Toni murmured excitedly. "Fans."

A small group of people stood near the door, holding their programs and asking for autographs from cast members.

"Look at Mark," Gillian whispered, pointing

to the tall, black-haired star of the show. "He's such a total ham."

Signing his name with a flourish, Mark Simmons returned a program to a young girl. Then he bowed from the waist and kissed the back of her hand. The girl blushed and giggled with her friends, who held out their own programs and squealed Mark's name.

"I don't know why he wastes his time," Liz said. "I mean, they can't do anything for his career."

"Honestly, Liz," Janna said, annoyed. "He's having fun. What do you care?"

Liz shot her a look, but didn't reply. And Janna noticed that when the small crowd spotted the four dancers and started asking for their autographs, Liz didn't refuse.

In her room at home, Janna had a collection of autographed programs, including one with Mikhail Baryshnikov's signature. The famous ballet dancer had given her a warm smile when he'd signed his name for her. Janna had been eight and never forgotten it.

She knew some people had a problem with signing autographs. Thought it was an invasion of their privacy or something. But Janna enjoyed it. It made her feel famous already and it made people happy.

Smiling, she took the program and a pen from a guy about her age. "What's your name?" she asked him.

The guy blushed. He was tall, with a thin face and shining blue eyes. "Um," he said. "It's Stan."

"Nice to meet you." Janna smiled again as she got ready to write in the program. "How'd you like the show?"

Stan finally found his voice. "It was great. *You* were great, Miss Richards. I'll bet you've been dancing since you were about five."

"Thanks," Janna said. "Six, actually." She wrote *Best wishes to Stan, from Janna Richards*, then handed back the program.

Stan kept looking at her, his gaze so admiring that Janna began to feel uncomfortable. Finally she turned away and bumped into a girl with soft, light brown hair.

"Stan, what's taking so long?" the girl asked in a complaining voice as she brushed past Janna. "I've been waiting at the car forever."

"Sorry." Stan kept watching Janna. "Oh, Janna," Stan called out. "I'd like you to meet my girlfriend, Carly. Carly, this is Janna Richards."

Janna turned around and threw Carly a friendly smile.

Carly didn't smile back. She slipped her arm through Stan's and looked up at him. "What's taking you so long?" she repeated, tucking a strand of hair behind her ear. "I thought we were going to get something to eat."

"We are," Stan told her. "I just wanted to get some of the stars' autographs. I told you that."

Carly finally looked at Janna. "What's your name again?" she demanded.

"Janna. And I'm not a star," Janna added with a laugh.

"I didn't think so." Carly tugged on Stan's arm. "Can we go now? I'm starving!"

As Carly dragged Stan off toward the parking lot, Janna glanced at Toni, who'd been standing nearby.

" 'I didn't think so,' " Toni said, mimicking Carly's tone. "What a snot! Someday, she'll be begging for your autograph."

Janna laughed. "Right. And I won't give her the time of day. Come on, let's get back to the motel. I'm wiped out."

As she moved on, Janna felt someone's eyes on her. She glanced back.

In the parking lot, Carly was climbing into a car.

But Stan was standing at the driver's door,

watching Janna, his eyes glittering in the parking lot light.

Janna waited for him to get in the car. But he continued to stare at her. That uneasy feeling came back. Forget it, she told herself.

But then she remembered what Stan had said. "You were great, Miss Richards."

And he'd said it before she signed the program.

Janna didn't have a name in the musical. She was just listed as one of the dancers.

How did he know her name?

Chapter 3

"I'm serious, Janna," Gillian said as they entered their motel room later. "If that guy shows up again, I'd call the police if I were you."

"And say what?" Liz snorted. " 'Stan the Fan knew my name before I signed his program?' Give it a rest, Gillian. He could have asked an usher for her name."

"I didn't think of that," Janna admitted, putting the roses on the crowded dresser top.

"And besides," Liz continued, "I thought you said your boyfriend sent the roses."

"*Ex*-boyfriend," Janna replied. "And I don't know what I'm saying, okay?"

"Well, don't get mad at me," Liz snapped. "*I* didn't send the roses."

"Yeah, but someone did," Gillian declared.

"Maybe it was Janna's ex or maybe this other guy. All I'm saying is she should be careful. Someone might be stalking her."

"*Stalking* her?" Liz said in disbelief. "Sending roses is not stalking someone. Last time I looked, it wasn't even a crime." She kicked off her shoes and pulled the rubber band from her hair. "Personally, Gillian, I think you've been reading too much tabloid trash."

"Well, personally, Liz, I don't care what you think." Gillian turned over and sat up. "Stalkers are not a joke. I read about this guy who sent candy and flowers at first, then dead insects. Then a rat — with its head chopped off."

"Oh, gross," Toni said.

"Give me a break!" Liz cried. "You guys are being paranoid. We're in the theater. Fans send roses and cards saying 'I love you' and 'Please marry me.' It happens all the time."

"I think Liz is right," Toni said.

"I *know* I'm right."

"Yeah, I guess I'm overreacting," Janna agreed.

"Anyway," Toni pointed out, "we'll be out of this town soon and it'll all be over."

"Speaking of towns, I hope the next one has

a better motel," Liz grumbled. She shook out her long blond hair and glanced around. "This place is the pits."

Glad for a change of subject, Janna followed Liz's gaze. The room had faded yellow walls, carpet the color of mud, curtains that didn't close all the way, lumpy beds, a tiny bathroom.

And no room service.

That's life on the road, Janna thought. So get used to it.

"Who gets the shower first?" Toni asked. They rotated every day.

"I do," Janna said. "But somebody can go ahead of me. I want to call home first."

Janna's parents and two older sisters — one married, one in college — thought the theater tour was incredibly exciting and had made her promise to call or write as often as possible.

Janna was pulling on her robe when the phone rang. Liz grabbed it on her way to the bathroom, listened a moment, and held the receiver out. "For you, Janna." She raised her eyebrows. "Male. A sexy voice. Know anybody like that?"

Janna took the phone. "Hello?"

"Hey, Janna."

The voice was sexy, but Janna didn't melt. It was Jimmy Dare's voice.

"You there, babe?" he asked.

"I'm here, Jimmy," Janna said. She thought again of the ugly drawing she'd gotten. "I got your message."

A pause. Then Jimmy laughed. "I didn't send a message. I started to, but I decided to call instead."

"Sure," Janna said. Liz had gone into the bathroom, but hadn't closed the door, she noticed. Gillian and Toni were sitting cross-legged on one of the beds, watching her. She rolled her eyes at them.

"Anyway, listen to *this* message," Jimmy continued. "I want us to make up." His voice was like silk. "Remember how great things could be between us?"

"Actually, I remember the fights better," Janna told him.

"Hey, don't be like that," he said. "Be nice."

Sure, Janna thought. Be nice. Be pretty.

Be mine.

When Janna didn't say anything, Jimmy spoke again. "Listen, babe, I know I got pretty wild when you took off with that show, but that's behind us now."

Janna sighed. "Jimmy, I'll still be in the show. And I'm majoring in theater in college. And after that . . . it's what I want to do with my life, and you just don't seem to get that."

"I get it now," he said, much too quickly.

"No, you don't," Janna said. "If you did, you wouldn't have sent me that drawing."

"What drawing?"

"Oh, come on, Jimmy." Janna sighed again. "Will you please drop the innocent act? The cute little drawing of a bloody, broken leg. Does that ring a bell?"

"Okay, okay, I sent it," Jimmy admitted. "I'm sorry, Jan." His voice was soft and sincere. "It was a joke."

"It was sick," Janna retorted.

"Look, I was angry. It was a stupid thing to do and I'm not proud of myself." Jimmy sounded impatient now. "I'm sorry. There — I've said it twice. Happy?"

"No, Jimmy. I'm not happy."

Janna glanced at Liz, who was in the bathroom doorway now, obviously enjoying the soap opera.

"Listen, Jimmy," Janna continued, turning her back on Liz. "We've been through this before, remember? We fight, we make up, we fight again. Getting back together won't work, Jimmy. It just won't work. It would be the biggest mistake of my life."

"Wrong, babe." The silkiness in Jimmy's

voice had totally disappeared. It was rough now. Not loud, but low and threatening. "What you just said about not getting back together — *that's* the biggest mistake of your life. Count on it."

"Is that a threat?"

"No, Janna, it's not a threat." Jimmy's voice became even more menacing. "It's a promise."

Chapter 4

"I don't believe it!" Furious, Janna slammed the phone down and blew out a big breath. "That guy is such a jerk! How could I have ever thought I cared about him? I must have been totally out of my mind!"

"What'd he say?" Toni asked. "What was that about him threatening you?"

"He said I'd regret not getting back together with him," Janna fumed. "Only according to him, it was a promise, not a threat."

"Sounds like he already did threaten you with that break-a-leg drawing," Gillian told her. "Did he admit that he sent it?"

"Finally," Janna said. "He said he was sorry."

"Maybe he is." Toni slid off the bed. "And then maybe he felt guilty and sent the roses.

You said he does things like that."

"Jimmy didn't feel one bit guilty, Toni," Janna said. "Actually, I didn't get to ask him about the roses. He's playing a game. And now he's mad again because I won't play along with him."

Toni looked concerned. "Well, if he's as mad as he sounds, then you ought to watch out for him."

Remembering the ugly tone of Jimmy's voice, Janna shivered slightly. "I'll be careful," she agreed. "But he's fifty miles away. I hope. Besides, he's never hurt me except with words. He's all talk."

"Don't be so sure," Liz told her. She was still standing in the bathroom doorway. "He sounds like a ticking bomb to me."

"Now who's being paranoid?" Janna asked. "Anyway, I'm sick of the subject of Jimmy Dare. Let's talk about something interesting. Like Ryan Mitchell."

"Ooh, a *very* interesting subject." Toni's eyes sparkled, as she shrugged into a short terry-cloth robe. "He's really cute, isn't he?"

"He's kind of quiet, though," Gillian said. "He sort of keeps to himself."

"That's part of the attraction," Janna said.

"What's his story, anyway?" She looked at Liz. "You were both in the company last summer, right?"

Liz nodded.

"Well?" Janna asked. "What's he like? Did you get to know him?"

"Yeah." Liz's mouth twisted in a small smile. "You could say that."

Uh-oh, Janna thought. Did Liz have a thing for Ryan, too? "Sounds like there's some history between you two," she said cautiously. She hoped is *was* history.

Liz didn't say anything for a moment. Then she crossed to the empty bed and sat down on it. "You're right," she told Janna. "There's definitely some history between me and Ryan Mitchell."

Liz's mouth twisted again. This time, the smile was bitter.

Liz took a deep breath. "Okay, here goes," she said. "When I first saw Ryan, I was really attracted. I could tell he was, too, because he kept looking at me. You know, at rehearsals, or when I'd be waiting to go on or something. I'd glance around and there he was, staring at me. Then he'd smile, like there was a secret between us. Mr. Mysterious, right? Very fascinating."

"You don't sound fascinated anymore," Toni said, sitting down next to Gillian.

"You're right about that," Liz agreed. "But I was then. Anyway, we started seeing each other. And . . ." She paused, smiling bitterly again.

"And?" Toni said eagerly. "What happened?"

"I fell in love," Liz said.

"What's so awful about that?" Gillian demanded.

"Don't you get it?" Liz asked. "I was in love. I thought Ryan was, too. I thought he really cared. And then he dropped me for another girl. And then he dropped *her* for somebody else. He'd probably forgotten my name by then. But I never forgot him."

Janna stared at her. It was hard to imagine icy Liz Thompson falling in love and getting her heart broken. But that was last summer, she reminded herself. Maybe she hadn't been so icy until Ryan dumped her.

If he dumped her, she thought.

"When I found out he was seeing somebody else, I asked him about it, which was really stupid," Liz went on. "He actually laughed. 'Hey, you know what life on the road is like,' he said. 'People come together, it's hot for a while and then it cools off.' "

"So what are you saying?" Janna asked. "Ryan's Mr. Heartbreaker and I should stay away from him?"

"It's up to you. But if you're smart, yeah, I think you should stay away from him." Liz stood up and headed for the bathroom again. Pausing in the doorway, she turned around. "But if you don't, just be careful. Ryan Mitchell puts on a nice act, but that's all it is. An act."

Janna came out of the steamy bathroom and glanced around. It was after midnight and her roommates were already asleep. Janna knew she should get in bed, too. They had rehearsal in the morning and another performance tomorrow night.

Moving quietly, she crossed the dim room to the dresser and reached for her bottle of hand lotion. The roses were still there, still in their green tissue paper. As she rubbed the lotion onto her legs, she could smell the strong, sweet scent of the flowers.

Soon you'll be mine. Soon, Janna.

Jimmy Dare was becoming a real pain. Frowning, Janna turned her back on the flowers and got into bed. She stuck her hand under the pillow and pulled out a small stuffed bear, a gift from her family. They'd given it to her when she was ten and had played the part of an orphan in a local production of *Oliver.*

She'd named it "Bearyshnikov," and had kept it with her ever since for good luck.

Lying back, Janna rubbed the bear's worn fur and stared at the cracked ceiling.

She should never have brought the flowers back with her.

She wanted their sickening smell and their blood-red blossoms out of the room. Out of her sight.

Getting up, she pulled on her blue cotton robe and slid into some flip-flops. She picked up the roses, got her key and some money, and left the room.

Outside, Janna walked quickly down the open-air corridor to the soda machine. She tossed the flowers into a large trash barrel, then fed some change into the machine and punched the button for a diet 7UP. The can thumped down noisily.

Except for a car parked in the empty lot across the street, the area was deserted. The night was quiet and the cool night air felt good. She popped the tab on the soda and took a long drink.

Leaning against the machine, she stared

across the street, thinking about Ryan Mitchell and Jimmy Dare.

Jimmy had been a major mistake.

If she ever got anything going with Ryan, would he turn out to be a mistake, too?

Janna closed her eyes and pictured Ryan's face. His gold-flecked eyes and his slow smile were definitely attractive.

It bothered Gillian the way he kind of kept to himself and didn't talk much, but Janna liked it. A lot of theater people were always "on." Ryan stood out just by being quiet.

According to Liz, though, it was all an act.

You can't believe everything you hear, Janna told herself. Especially if it comes from Liz Thompson. Every story has two sides. Find out what Ryan's side is.

Reaching up, Janna felt her hair to see if it was dry.

Across the street, a car's headlights burst on, trapping Janna like a deer in the bright glare of the high beams.

Startled, she waited for the car to pull away.

It didn't move.

Janna shaded her eyes. In the dim glow of a streetlight, she could just make out the dark shape of the driver.

Motionless, like the car.

Janna tightened her grip on the soda can.

A car with its headlights, focused on her. A motionless, faceless driver.

Watching her?

It felt the same. Someone watching her, hidden behind a glaring light. First at the theater. Now at the motel.

Janna tossed the soda can into the trash barrel and ran down the walkway.

When she reached her room, she nervously fumbled with the key, her heart pounding.

Was he out of his car, crossing the street? Coming after her?

At last, she got the door open and slipped inside, locking the door behind her.

Taking a deep breath, she began to calm down. Was it Jimmy?

Anger replaced her fear. Janna unlocked the door and stepped out, ready to really give it to him.

But the parking lot across the street was empty now.

He was gone.

But for how long?

Chapter 5

"Okay, everybody, from the top."

Pacing around the stage like a panther, Gray Williams took the dancers through part of the "Hand Jive" number, where the kids at *Grease*'s Rydell High competed in a dance contest.

The stage was crowded and the timing was tricky. Janna hoped everybody got it right this time. They'd been working on it for an hour and Gray still wasn't satisfied.

Counting the beats in her head, she ran across the stage and grabbed Eric's outstretched hands, then slid between his legs and hopped up again. Facing each other, they went into a fast, furious jitterbug.

On the scaffold high above the stage, a lighting man pulled the filter from one of the spotlights. White light flashed across Janna's face, bringing back the memory of last night.

The parked car.

The motionless driver.

The headlights pinning her in their glare.

"Come on, Richards!" Eric hissed as Janna almost missed a step. "Concentrate or we'll be here 'til curtain time."

"Sorry," Janna whispered.

Get a grip, she told herself.

As the dance ended, Eric knelt down. Janna stepped onto his knee and sat on his shoulder, one arm flung above her head. They held the pose, smiles pasted across their faces, their breath coming heavily.

"Better," Gray said. "Let's get it right tonight, too. See you then."

Relieved, the dancers scattered from the stage. It was lunchtime and they were free until six, when they had to return and get ready for the night's performance.

In the dressing room, Janna peeled out of her sweaty leotard and pulled on a pair of cut-off jeans and a white T-shirt. Gillian and Toni were on their way to a movie and asked her along, but Janna decided not to go. "I'm out of toothpaste and shampoo and a hundred other things," she told them. "Besides, I'm starving. Popcorn won't be enough."

In a drugstore on Main Street, Janna bought her supplies and a bag of mini candy bars for motel room munching. As she came out of the store and headed down the sidewalk, someone grabbed her shoulder from behind.

Janna gasped and spun around.

Ryan Mitchell stood there, smiling at her. "What's the matter, did I scare you?" he asked.

Janna let her breath out in relief. "Hi, Ryan. I am a little jumpy, I guess."

"What about?"

"It's kind of strange. But I feel like . . ." Janna hesitated, not wanting to mention Jimmy Dare. ". . . like I'm being watched by somebody."

"Guilty," Ryan said quickly. Then he laughed. "I've been watching you since the first day I saw you."

He laughed again, and the gold flecks in his eyes sparkled. A dimple Janna had never noticed before appeared in his cheek. She found herself smiling back. "I didn't notice that," she told him.

"You mean I was too subtle?" Ryan shook his head. "Okay, I'll spell it out." He nodded toward a restaurant a couple of doors down.

"I'd like to get to know you, Janna. How about having lunch with me?"

Janna didn't hesitate. If Ryan was Mr. Heartbreaker, like Liz said, there was only one way to find out. "Let's eat," she agreed.

Later, after Janna had plowed her way through a salad, a turkey sandwich, and a piece of apple pie, Ryan cocked an eyebrow at her empty plates. "Does stage fright kill your appetite or something?" he asked teasingly.

"I did kind of pig out, didn't I?" Janna admitted, stirring the straw in her soda. "But lunch is the only chance I get. If I stuff myself right before a show, I'll fall asleep in the middle of it."

"So you don't get stage fright?"

"Oh, sure I do," Janna said. "I'm terrified every time I go out there." She drank some Coke and leaned her elbows on the table. "Okay, Ryan. I've told you everything about myself, including the time I threw up before my first dance recital. It's your turn now."

"You want the Ryan Mitchell Story, huh?" Ryan closed his eyes. "Let's see. I was born nineteen years ago, on a rainy night in March. The temperature was . . ."

Janna laughed and tossed her wadded-up napkin at him. "I don't want to know *that* much," she said. "Where are you from? Do you have any brothers or sisters? How'd you get involved in the theater?"

Do you have a girlfriend? she thought but didn't say.

"Wisconsin. One brother in medical school," Ryan said. "And I volunteered to paint sets for *Carousel* my sophomore year in high school," he told her. "After that I was hooked. I still am. I hope I can keep getting work."

"Doing what?"

Ryan shrugged. "That, I don't know. I get to direct a one-act play in college this year, so I'll see how that goes. But I like the backstage work, too, especially lighting and scenery. This is my third summer with this theater company."

"You never wanted to act or dance or anything?"

"I'd love to," Ryan said. "There's just one problem."

"What?"

"No talent. If I ever make my mark in theater, it won't be onstage, that's for sure." He shrugged again, laughing.

Janna grinned. "You're the first nonobsessive theater person I've met, Ryan."

He raised a sandy eyebrow. "Obsessive?"

"You know what I mean," Janna told him. "So many of us live and breathe acting or dancing. We don't have room in our lives for anything else."

"Well, I really want to work in it, but I guess you're right," he agreed. "I'm not *obsessed* with it. I'm interested in other things, too."

"Like what?"

"Oh . . . skiing. Science." Ryan cleared his throat and sipped some water. "And you," he said, blushing a little. "I'm interested in you, Janna."

Janna's heart thumped and she felt a warm rush of pleasure.

Was he acting? He said he couldn't, but this wasn't a stage.

And if it was an act, it was a good one.

"No wonder you didn't want to go to the movies with us, Janna," Toni said teasingly. "You had something much more exciting to do."

"I didn't know it was going to happen," Janna protested with a laugh. She'd met up with Toni and Gillian after leaving Ryan, and now the three of them were heading back to the motel.

"But you're right, having lunch with Ryan Mitchell was definitely more exciting than seeing a movie."

Gillian frowned. "I take it you've forgotten what Liz said about him."

"I haven't forgotten," Janna said thoughtfully. "But I don't intend to let something Liz said scare me off. Would you, Gill?"

"Probably not right away," Gillian admitted. "But I'd be careful."

"Lighten up, Gillian!" Toni gave her a playful shove. "You're always *so* serious."

"Right," Janna agreed. "Besides, all I did was have lunch with him."

"You mean things didn't get hot and heavy over sandwiches and Cokes?" Toni asked.

"No." As they turned toward the motel, Janna grinned. "They got warm, though."

In the motel room, they found Liz taking a nap on one of the beds. An envelope and three phone messages for Janna were on the dresser.

All three phone calls were from Jimmy Dare. *Will call back,* they said.

Janna wadded them up and tossed them into the wastepaper basket. You're wasting your time, Jimmy, she thought.

While Toni took a shower and Gillian tiptoed

around, gathering a bundle of dirty clothes for the launderette, Janna stretched out on her bed and opened the envelope.

As she read the typewritten letter, Janna's heart began to pound. Not with pleasure, the way it had with Ryan, but with terror.

I dreamed about you last night, Janna. You were dancing, the way you were when I first saw you. As I stood and watched you, I felt this incredible urge to touch you. So I held out my hands.

You know what happened, Janna? You came running to me! You jumped into my arms and kissed me. Your black hair smelled like flowers and your skin felt like silk.

It was the best dream I ever had.

And some day soon, I'll make it come true.

I know it's too soon for you to be dreaming of me. But you will, Janna. You will.

A fan.

P.S. You shouldn't have thrown the roses away! How do you think that made me feel? Furious, Janna. So furious, I almost forgot how much I love you!

Chapter 6

"I already told you a hundred times," Liz said in the dressing room that evening. "When I got back to the motel, I stopped at the desk for messages. The guy handed them to me and I put them on the dresser." She leaned close to the mirror and began lining her eyes with black pencil. "I didn't know this would turn into a federal case, so excuse me if I didn't ask him who delivered the envelope."

"Well, it wasn't the mailman, that's for sure," Gillian said, tying a yellow ribbon around her ponytail. "There was no stamp. And that means he's right here in town. How else did he know Janna threw away the roses? He sat across the street last night and watched her do it."

"Let's stop talking about it," Janna said. She

dropped a blue-striped dress over her puffy crinoline slip. "I'd like to put the whole thing out of my mind before we go on. I can't let Jimmy Dare freak me out so much that I blow it onstage."

"Quiet, everybody," Liz said sarcastically. "Janna's trying to get into character."

Janna shot her a look, but didn't comment. She was already nervous. Fighting with Liz wouldn't help.

In silence, the dancers finished getting into costume and applying their makeup. As Janna outlined her lips with red, someone rapped on the door.

"Twenty minutes," Ryan's voice announced.

"Thank you!" Toni shouted. "How's the house?"

"Filling up," Ryan said. "Is Janna in there?"

Toni caught Janna's eye and wiggled her eyebrows. "Yes she is!" she sang out. "Would you like to see her again?"

"Again?" Liz glanced curiously at Janna.

"Yeah, Janna, do you have a second?" Ryan called out.

Ignoring Liz's questioning look, Janna threaded her way through the narrow dressing room and stepped outside.

"Hi, Ryan, what's up?" she asked, closing the door behind her.

"Nothing major." Ryan smiled. "I have to make an emergency run to the hardware store in a few minutes and I'll be staying on after the show to help with some set repairs," he explained. "Anyway, since I might not get another chance to talk to you, I wanted to make sure you knew about tomorrow night's party."

Janna nodded. There was usually a cast party after every closing, and this one was in a club not far from her motel. "I saw the announcement yesterday," she told Ryan.

"Are you going?" he asked.

"Sure."

"Great. I was hoping you were." Ryan seemed to hesitate. Then he reached out and smoothed a strand of Janna's hair away from her face. His hand dropped to her shoulder and stayed there.

Janna's heart picked up its pace as Ryan leaned close to her. "Gotta run," he murmured, his breath tickling her ear.

And then he was gone.

Janna took a deep breath. Don't get wobbly-legged now, she thought, grinning to herself. At least wait until the show's over!

* * *

Ten minutes to curtain.

In front of a stack of painted flats, Janna did a few knee bends and leg stretches to limber up. She could hear the audience out front, rustling their programs and greeting each other. In a few more minutes, the band would begin tuning up.

Janna's heart started pounding and her hands shook with the rush of adrenaline that always hit her just before curtain.

She was taking a few deep breaths, trying to calm down, when she saw Vic, the stage manager, hurrying toward her.

"Phone call, Janna," Vic said. "Sounds important. Know where the phone is?"

Janna knew. Rushing downstairs and along the hall that led to the theater manager's office, she could only think of one reason why Vic would let her take a call eight minutes before curtain: Something must have happened at home.

Something bad.

Passing the dressing rooms, Janna turned a corner and ran to the end of the hall, into the office. The phone's receiver lay on top of a stack of papers. She grabbed it up.

"Hello?" she said breathlessly. "Mom . . . Dad?"

"No, Janna." The voice was low and muffled. "Don't worry — nothing's wrong. I had to do some lying, but it was worth it, don't you think?"

"Who *is* this?" Janna cried. "Is this . . ."

"You know who I am, Janna," the voice interrupted. "I'm your biggest fan."

"My fan." Janna's hand was suddenly slick with sweat and she almost dropped the phone. "Jimmy?"

The caller laughed softly. "Didn't you get my letter?"

"Oh, yeah, I got it," Janna said. "I got the roses, too. Listen . . ."

"Yes, the roses. You threw them away."

Janna felt a surge of anger. "You wouldn't know that if you hadn't been spying on me!"

"I love to watch you. Don't you get it?"

"No," Janna said coldly.

"Trust me, you will. Soon."

"Stop saying that!" Janna shouted. "Leave me alone, Jimmy!"

With another soft laugh, the caller hung up.

"I warned you," Liz reminded Janna in the motel room later that night. "Didn't I say Gray would jump all over you if you made a single mistake?"

"Yes, Liz, you told me. Thanks a lot for reminding me," Janna said sarcastically. "I feel so much better now."

"Hey, I didn't mean it like that," Liz protested as she toweled her hair dry.

Sure you didn't, Janna thought.

"Actually, I was trying to cheer you up," Liz continued. "Except for Eric, nobody else but Gray noticed that you missed all those steps in the opening number. That's what I meant — he's such a perfectionist, he sees every picky little thing. Try not to let him get you down."

Sure, Janna thought again. Gray had only chewed her out in front of a dozen people. It was impossible not to feel down about something like that.

"Did you explain what happened, Janna?" Gillian asked. "About the call and everything?"

"I started to, but he didn't want to hear it." Janna sat on the bed and reached for Baryshnikov. "He just said I shouldn't have taken a call so close to curtain, and then he walked away."

"Try not to feel so bad," Toni said sympathetically, as she got into bed. "If I'd gotten a call like that, I wouldn't even have made it onstage. I don't know how you managed to dance at all after what he said to you."

"It was awful," Janna agreed. "He's starting to drive me nuts! Flowers and letters and now a call. Jimmy's going over the edge. I don't know what he'll try next!" She shoved her pillow against the headboard and leaned back. "I've tried to tell him how I feel, but it's like he doesn't even hear me."

"Crazies like this don't care how their victims feel," Gillian said. "They say they do, but all they really care about is themselves."

Victim.

It sounded so weak. Helpless, Janna thought. And she'd never felt weak or helpless in her life. She'd fight, if only Jimmy would show his face.

"He's obsessed," Gillian went on, climbing into the other bed. "Telling him to stop won't work."

"So what am I supposed to do?" Janna cried.

"I say go to the police," Toni declared.

"Time out, guys," Liz interrupted. "I still say you're all overreacting."

"You didn't hear him on the phone, Liz," Janna pointed out. "I did. Whispering so I wouldn't recognize his voice."

"Whispering?" Toni said. "Are you positive it was Jimmy?"

Janna thought a moment. "Not completely," she admitted.

"Who else could it be?" Gillian asked.

Toni sat up and wrapped her arms around her knees. "I hate to say this, but I was talking with some of the crew and . . ." she hesitated and took a deep breath. "Well, this girl named Kathy Kramer — she was just starting to make it on Broadway when she was brutally murdered. They never caught the killer."

"People do get murdered in New York, you know," Liz pointed out. "What does that have to do with Janna?"

"The papers said she was the victim of a stalker. A fan." Toni bit her lip. "And before she went to New York, Kathy Kramer was in *this* theater company!"

Brutally murdered.
The victim of a stalker.
The words kept spinning through Janna's mind as she tried to go to sleep. Shivering,

she tugged up the cover and rolled over.

She was on the side of the bed nearest the window. Through the gap in the drooping curtain, she could see the hazy light from the moon. She shut her eyes against it.

Almost immediately, she began thinking about her "biggest fan." His call, his words, had made her so nervous she'd messed up in the show. She couldn't let that happen again, but she didn't know how to stop it. *Was* it Jimmy? Or someone else? Would he ever leave her alone?

Kathy Kramer's "fan" hadn't. Not until she'd been brutally murdered.

Brutally murdered.

Squeezing her eyes tight, Janna tried to shut the words out of her mind.

Think about Ryan Mitchell, she told herself. Picture his face. Remember the way he brushed your hair back. How warm his breath felt when he whispered in your ear.

It didn't work. The memory of the caller kept intruding. Shattering Ryan's image with his eerie, muffled voice.

How would she ever get to sleep?

Sighing, Janna decided to get up. Maybe a drink of water would help.

As she swung her legs over the side of the

bed, her stuffed bear tumbled to the floor. Janna reached down to pick him up.

And froze in terror.

Through the gap in the curtain, two eyes peered into the room.

Two eyes, focused hungrily on Janna's face.

Chapter 7

Janna screamed, jumping toward the window. "Get away and leave me alone!"

The eyes disappeared. Janna tore the curtains apart and screamed again. "What do you think you're doing? Leave me alone! You hear me?" She pounded her fist on the window.

Behind her, the others jumped from their beds, asking startled questions. Janna ignored them. She pressed her face close to the window, cupping her eyes to see better.

Somebody running off. Just a shadow, but definitely human. Running along the wall and around the corner. Out of sight.

"Who was it?" Toni cried. "Was it Jimmy?"

"I don't know!" Janna whirled around and raced for the door. "But he was outside the window, staring in at me. Come on!"

"Are you out of your mind?" Gillian shouted,

blocking the door. "You can't go running after him!"

"She's right, Janna," Toni said. "It's too dangerous."

Janna's arms shook with anger and fear, but she moved away from the door. Toni was right — it would be stupid to go chasing after him.

Gillian was on the phone. Cupping her hand over the mouthpiece, she turned to Janna. "The desk manager says he'll take a look around outside. He also wants to know if we want the police."

"For what?" Liz asked skeptically. "He's blocks away by now. Probably miles."

"Janna?" Gillian asked.

Janna shook her head. Liz was right, unfortunately. It was too late for the police. All she could say was that she saw a pair of eyes.

Hungry eyes, watching her.

"A 7UP!" Janna shouted over the throbbing bass of the music blasting from the wall speakers. "With a slice of lime!"

The bartender at The Neon Palace finally heard her. Nodding, he poured the soda over ice, added the lime, and set the glass in front of her. "You're with the theater group, right? *Grease?*"

"Right." Janna paid for the drink and took a sip. "How'd you know?"

"Lucky guess." The bartender chuckled. "A lot of you are here tonight. Great for business."

Janna picked up her soda and glanced around.

The Neon Palace was a huge, cavernous place. Tubes of purple and red neon zigzagged up the walls and across the ceiling. Strobe lights flickered across the bodies of couples dancing in the center of the big wooden floor. Waiters in red and purple shirts rushed around, carrying food to the small, crowded tables set against the walls.

Most of the theater company was here, like the bartender said. Dancing, eating. Laughing loudly. Tonight's performance had been great. A sold-out house. No missed cues. No sour notes. Plenty of curtain calls. Tomorrow, they'd set out for another town. Tonight, they partied.

Sipping her 7UP, Janna narrowed her eyes and let her gaze travel from face to face. Trying to catch someone watching her. She'd been like this all day. Edgy. Looking over her shoulder.

At least she hadn't let last night affect her

performance. But now, when she should be partying with everyone else, she was standing on the sidelines.

Looking for a stalker.

An arm slid around her shoulder and Janna jumped, almost dropping her glass.

"Whoa," Ryan said with a smile. "Didn't mean to scare you."

Janna let her breath out. "Hi, Ryan. I'm glad you're here."

"Me, too. I would have been here sooner, but we had a few problems breaking down the set." He pulled back and looked at her, his green eyes lighting up. "You look great, Janna. Not that you look bad in a fifties dress, but this one's definitely more your style."

Janna laughed. She wore a red dress with almost no back. Her black hair was loose, with two sparkling combs pulling it away from her face.

"Thanks, Ryan," she said. "Come on. Let's dance." Taking his hand, she led him away from the bar and into the middle of the dance floor.

Maybe dancing would make her forget the stalker.

After three fast dances, the music switched to a slow number. Ryan slipped his arm around

Janna's waist and pulled her close to him.

Janna took a deep breath. Ryan smelled of shampoo and aftershave, and his shirt was a silvery-gray cotton. She rubbed her fingers across the soft fabric, then leaned her cheek against it.

"Janna," he murmured.

"Mmm?" She was finally starting to relax.

"Being on the road is dangerous, you know."

"Dangerous? What do you mean?" She glanced up, startled.

Ryan smiled. "A dangerous place for people to fall in love," he said. "I mean, what happens when the tour's over?"

Janna shook her head. "They write. They try to get together. Why? Who's in love?"

"I'm not sure." Ryan stopped dancing. "But I think I could be," he whispered. "Soon."

Soon.

Janna tensed up at the word.

"Hey, what's wrong?" Ryan asked. "That wasn't just a line, you know. Janna?"

The music started up again, fast and loud this time. Throbbing with a heavy beat.

It was impossible to talk, so Janna danced, hoping to wear out her nerves. She and Ryan danced through three more songs, and then she fanned herself with her hand. "Gotta get some water on my face or I'll melt," she said.

"Okay. I'll get us something to drink." Cupping her face with both hands, Ryan kissed her quickly. "I wanted to do that before," he said with a grin. Then he headed for the bar.

Smiling to herself, Janna was making her way toward the bathroom when she shivered suddenly, in spite of the heat.

Eyes on her. Looking at her.

She knew the feeling well by now.

Someone was watching her.

Get a grip, she told herself. Look at this place — it's packed. Hundreds of people could be watching you. Maybe they are. After all, you look pretty good tonight.

Still, at the edge of the dance floor, Janna stopped and glanced around.

Gillian, dancing with Eric, wasn't even looking her way.

She couldn't spot Toni anywhere.

But Ryan was glancing at her from the bar.

And standing next to Ryan, frowning across the room at Janna, was Liz Thompson.

Catching Janna's eye, Liz looked away.

"Excuse me. Janna?" a voice said.

Janna turned quickly.

A tall guy stood just behind her. Next to

him was a girl with soft, wispy brown hair. The guy's hair was brown, too, and his face was thin. He had blue eyes.

Shining blue eyes.

Janna shivered.

Hadn't she seen those eyes before?

Chapter 8

The guy smiled shyly at her.

As Janna stared at him, his face began to turn pink and his smile faltered a little. "I guess you don't remember me," he said.

Oh, but I do, Janna thought, not taking her eyes from his. Stan . . . the fan.

"Look, Carly. It's Janna Richards."

The brown-haired girl standing nearby turned around. "Who?"

"Janna Richards," Stan told her. "From *Grease*. We saw her the other night."

Carly shrugged. "If you say so, Stan."

"Remember me now?" Stan asked Janna.

"Sure," she said slowly. Of course she did. Stan the Fan with the shining blue eyes and the uptight girlfriend. And here he was again, watching her. "I signed your program."

"That's right!" Stan said, looking flattered.

And you knew my name before I signed it, Janna thought.

Janna kept staring at him. Were those the same eyes that had watched her through the window last night?

Stan cleared his throat. "So," he said. "How's the show going?"

"Fine." Was that the voice on the phone? Janna couldn't tell. "We closed tonight," she said. "We're off to another town tomorrow morning."

"Come on, Stan," Carly said, nudging him. "I thought we came here to dance, not stand around and talk." She glanced around the room and sighed. "Not that we'll be able to dance. This place is so crowded I feel like a sardine!"

Carly tugged on his arm, but Stan didn't move. "It's really nice to see you again, Janna," he said. "Like I told you the other night, you're a great dancer."

"Thanks." Janna tried to smile but her face felt tight. Her whole body felt tight.

This could be the guy who was stalking her. Sending her roses. Calling her. Staring at her.

The way he'd stared at her last night through the motel room curtain.

The more she thought about it, the angrier she got.

"What made you decide to come here to-night?" Janna asked sharply.

"I . . . huh?" Stan looked surprised at her tone.

"I'll bet it was Stan's idea, wasn't it?" Janna asked Carly.

"So what if it was?" Carly said defensively. "What's your problem, anyway?"

Janna looked at Stan. "Did you know I'd be here?" she asked him. "Did you *call* the theater and find out where the cast party would be?"

Carly's gaze shifted from Janna to Stan. Back to Janna. "What's going on?" Carly asked, sounding annoyed and suspicious.

"Good question," Janna snapped. "Maybe Stan can answer it."

"Are you out of your mind?" Carly retorted.

Janna ignored her. "I'll bet this place has a pretty high cover charge, Stan. How'd you afford it after all those roses?"

"Roses?" Carly's face flushed angrily. "What's she talking about, Stan?"

"Go ahead, Stan. Tell her," Janna demanded.

"Tell me what?"

Stan's eyes were wide. He gulped. "I . . . I don't . . ." he stammered.

"Tell her, Stan. Tell her!" Janna insisted, raising her voice.

"Come on, Stan!" Carly urged, yanking at his arm. "Let's get away from this wacko!"

Suddenly Janna became aware that other people were around, watching the little scene she'd created. One of them was Liz, shaking her head in disgust.

Oh, no, what am I doing? Janna wondered. She had absolutely no proof that Stan was the stalker!

"Listen," she said quickly. "I'm sorry. I'm tired. Forget what I said."

"Oh, sure!" Carly said sarcastically. "And tell the other three hundred people in this room to forget it too. You're sick. Leave us alone."

Beet-red with embarrassment, Stan finally gave in to Carly's tugs. Janna watched them leave. Carly glared back at her as Stan murmured in her ear, obviously trying to explain something.

The little crowd of watchers broke up, leaving Janna by herself.

"Hey, what's the matter?" Ryan asked, coming up to her with a glass of Coke in each hand.

Janna gulped some soda. Her hands were shaking.

"You okay?" Ryan asked, looking concerned.

Janna shook her head, but she was too humiliated to tell him what had happened.

"What's wrong, Janna? Is there anything I can do?"

"Yeah, there is, Ryan." She took a deep breath. Tossed her hair back. "You can dance with me."

She swallowed the rest of her Coke, then hurried Ryan onto the dance floor. She loved to dance, anywhere. Onstage. In a club. On the street. It always made her feel great.

But now, not even dancing with Ryan Mitchell could make her feel good, not after what had just happened.

She couldn't stop wondering — had she just made a total fool of herself?

Or had she met the stalker face-to-face?

Still in her red dress, Janna fastened another safety pin in the motel room curtain. One more and the gap should be closed.

This was their last night in this place, but she wasn't taking any chances.

"You're definitely losing it, Janna," Liz remarked, coming out of the bathroom.

Toni glanced up from the duffel bag she was packing. "I think pinning that curtain's a good idea," she said. "Too bad we didn't do it before."

"I'm not talking about the curtain," Liz said. "I'm talking about the way Janna practically attacked that poor guy at the club tonight."

Gillian pulled on a short yellow bathrobe. "If he's the one who's been bothering her, then he deserved it."

"Yeah, but what if he wasn't?" Liz asked. "It's a good thing we're leaving tomorrow. He'd probably call the psycho ward, make them come pick her up. You should have seen the look on his face. *And* his girlfriend's face. Talk about embarrassed!"

"Why don't you rub it in, Liz?" Janna said.

"All I'm saying is . . ."

"All you're saying is I acted like an idiot," Janna interrupted. "Thank you very much. But even if I was wrong about him, it's over. We're leaving town. So why don't we just stop talking about him?"

Liz zipped her suitcase. "Fine," she said. "Want to talk about Ryan Mitchell instead? I notice you've decided not to take my advice about him."

Janna frowned and started to say something. Then she just smiled. She was feeling good now. Too good to let Liz get under her skin anymore.

It was after two in the morning. The buses left at eight. Janna hadn't packed. She hadn't even changed her clothes yet.

Sighing, she stuck the last safety pin in the curtain and stood up.

The others were almost finished packing. Better get to it, she told herself.

She slung a big duffel bag onto the bed and unzipped it. As she crossed to the dresser to get some clothes, there was a knock at the door.

Without even thinking, Janna opened it.

"I finally got you," Jimmy Dare said.

Chapter 9

"Jimmy!" Janna gasped. "What are you doing here?"

Jimmy's dark eyes raked her from head to foot. He gave her a slow smile. "Looking good, Janna!"

"I asked you a question," Janna reminded him.

"I heard you." Jimmy leaned against the door frame, stretching one arm up against it. His arm muscle swelled against the sleeve of his dark blue T-shirt. "I came to see you, Janna, what do you think I'm doing here?"

"That's nice, but you're too late," Janna told him. "The performance was over a long time ago."

"I wasn't interested in the show." He looked past her, into the room. "Aren't you going to invite me in?"

You wish, Janna thought. She glanced over her shoulder.

Her three roommates were standing like statues. Toni's mouth open in suprise. Gillian looking wary. Liz with a sly smile on her face.

Turning back to Jimmy, Janna said, "Come on. Let's talk outside."

Jimmy's eyes narrowed. He stared at her for a moment longer. Then he gave her a charming smile and a mock bow as he stepped back.

Janna went out, slamming the door behind her. "All right, Jimmy," she said, moving quickly down the dim corridor toward the front of the motel. "Could we make this fast? I have to pack and be on a bus at eight in the morning."

"Come on, Jan, don't be like this," he said. "I admit, I acted like a jerk, sending you that drawing. But I'm crazy about you, you know that."

Sighing, Janna leaned against the soda machine.

"Aren't you even a little bit impressed that I drove all this way to see you?" Jimmy asked with a grin. "Where've you been, anyway?"

When Janna didn't answer, Jimmy's grin disappeared. "Never mind," he said. "I already know."

Janna stared at him. What did he mean by that? Had he been at the club, spying on her?

"Now I see why you were so hot on going on this tour," he continued. "It's a great way for you to meet guys."

"You don't know what you're talking about," Janna said.

"Oh?" He cocked his head. Raised a dark eyebrow. "So why's your face all red? It matches that sexy dress, Janna. Is that the dress you wear to pack in or the one you used to attract some guy?"

Thinking of Ryan, Janna felt her face get even hotter.

"I'm right, aren't I?" Jimmy said. He took a step closer and put his hand on her arm. "But that's all over now, babe. That's why I'm here, to get you back where you belong. With me, Janna."

"You're crazy! I didn't go on this tour to meet guys!" Janna shouted. "You'll never understand why I joined the company — that's your whole problem!"

"Don't tell me I'm crazy, babe." Jimmy's voice was softer now. Dangerously soft.

"Then stop acting like it," Janna told him. "Barging in on me in the middle of the night. Checking up on me. Accusing me of things that aren't true." She took a deep breath. "And stop calling me babe!"

Jimmy just stared at her, his brown eyes narrowed.

"It's over, Jimmy," Janna said quietly. "*We're* over. I don't know how else to say it."

Jimmy still didn't say anything.

Janna took another deep breath, then stepped past him and started back to her room.

"Hey, Janna."

She turned around.

"Better watch yourself." Jimmy cocked his thumb, stuck his forefinger at her like the barrel of a gun. "*Babe.*"

Janna froze in her tracks. Jimmy Dare *was* the stalker. And he was going to keep at it — unless she stopped him.

"Jimmy! Listen and listen carefully," she said. "Leave me alone. No letters. No flow-flowers. No calls and no watching me. Stay out of my life or I'll make *your* life miserable!"

Jimmy started to say something but Janna

didn't give him a chance. Spinning on her heel, she left him without a backward glance.

The company left for Braxton shortly after eight the next morning. Janna dozed in the bus, waking once or twice to gaze down at fields of wheat and roadside vegetable stands. She was tired and groggy, but glad to be on the road.

She'd said good-bye to Jimmy Dare for the last time, she hoped. He was back home by now, with miles of highway between them.

As the bus rolled along, Janna felt better and better. Jimmy Dare was history.

"I don't believe it!" Gillian said loudly.

Janna jerked awake. The bus was pulling into the parking lot of a small, two-story cinder-block motel. Across the two-lane road was a junk shop and a telephone booth.

"Look!" Gillian said, nudging Janna in the side. "We've got a pool."

"Are you sure this is our motel?" Janna asked, looking at the small pool of bright blue water in front of the building.

Toni's red head appeared over the seatback in front. "You've been sleeping," she said to Janna. "The bus already dropped everybody else off at their motels. This one is definitely ours, and we've got a pool!"

"Now let's hope we've got air-conditioning," Liz added.

The room was larger than the last one, not quite as run-down, and the air conditioner was cold enough to bring the goose bumps out on Janna's bare arms.

She and her roommates dumped their luggage in their ground-floor room, then took their dance bags and left for the theater. Gray had called a ten o'clock rehearsal.

"As soon as we're free, I'm going back and jump in that water," Gillian declared. She lifted her hair off the back of her neck as they walked the quarter-mile to the theater.

"Maybe we can have a party," Janna suggested. She was already thinking of inviting Ryan. It would be great to swim with him. Lie in the sun with him.

Too bad they weren't staying at the same motel. There hadn't been enough room for the whole company.

Their walk took them past a small strip mall with a 7-Eleven, a beauty parlor, and a video-rental store. Past that was a graveled drive leading up to the Braxton Theater, a huge white building shaped like a barn. On the marquee, in big black letters, were the words, "Grease. A 50's Rock Musical. Regional Theater Company."

The girls followed the drive around back, where the company truck was pulled up to the open stage doors. Crew members were still unloading painted flats and racks of costumes.

Janna looked for Ryan, but didn't see him. Probably inside, she thought. She pushed her hair back and smiled in anticipation.

"Okay, everybody!" Vic, the stage manager, shouted as most of the cast gathered backstage. "Dancers! Girls' dressing room is Number Two, stage right, downstairs. Guys upstairs, stage left. Gray wants you onstage in fifteen minutes."

As Vic pointed out dressing rooms to the principal actors, Janna and her roommates headed downstairs.

"Another hole in the wall," Liz complained as they walked along a narrow, cement-floored hall to their dressing room.

Gillian rolled her eyes at Janna. "When you're famous, Liz, you can have your own private dressing room. With a Jacuzzi."

"It can't happen soon enough," Liz grumbled, opening the door marked "Number Two."

It was a narrow, windowless room with a long counter bolted to the wall. A long mirror ran above the counter, surrounded by bare lightbulbs.

"Look!" Toni cried, pointing to a small pile of envelopes on the counter. "Mail!" Toni dived for it and started handing it out. "Gillian, Liz. Me. Janna." She glanced up. "Janna?"

Janna took the letters Toni gave her, but didn't look at them. Her eyes were riveted to the far end of the dressing table, where a single rose stood in a green glass bud vase. A small white card was taped to the side of the vase.

"Oh, no," Toni breathed, following Janna's gaze. "I can't believe it."

Janna couldn't believe it, either.

Another rose.

Another sweet-smelling, blood-red rose.

"I thought it was over," Janna said, her voice shaking. "I thought it was . . . dump it!" she cried. "Just looking at it makes me sick. Somebody throw it in the garbage!"

"Wait a second!" Liz said, as Toni picked up the vase. "Maybe you're not curious about what he has to say, but I am."

Liz snatched the vase from Toni and ripped the little card off. As she read it, her mouth curled in a strange smile. "Yeah," she murmured. "This belongs in the garbage, all right."

Janna took a shaky breath. "All right, tell me. What'd he say this time?"

"*Janna,*" Liz read. "*Can't get you out of my mind. R.*"

"R?" Toni asked. "Oh! Ryan!"

"That's Ryan's style, all right," Liz said, turning away. "He's setting you up for a fall, Janna. Take my word for it."

But Janna barely heard Liz's warning. The rose was from Ryan. Laughing with relief, she took the rose from Liz and set it on the dressing table, then started changing her clothes.

During a break in rehearsal, Janna went looking for Ryan.

She finally spotted him high up on a scaffold, repairing a rip in one of the pieces of scenery. Quickly, she climbed up one end and poked her head over the top. "Hi, there. Got a second?"

Ryan grinned and scooted on his knees to the end of the scaffold. "For you? I can probably spare ten seconds."

Janna laughed. "I came to thank you for the

rose. It was really sweet of you. Freaked me out at first, but . . ."

"Freaked you out?" Ryan interrupted, confused.

"I thought it might be from some strange fan or something like that. But this rose, I like." Janna stretched up and kissed him quickly on the cheek. "Gotta go get a new shoelace. Gray wants us back in five and one of mine broke. See you later!"

Smiling to herself, Janna trotted downstairs and into the dressing room.

Her smile froze as she glanced at the mirror.

Then her lips twisted. Her mouth opened. She tried to scream, but no sound came out.

All she heard was her heart, thundering in her ears.

Scrawled across the mirror in blood-red lipstick — her lipstick — was a message:

Miss me yet? I'm closer than you think. We'll be together, Janna. Soon.

"No!" Janna shouted, furiously. "You're sick! Sick!" She grabbed her lipstick and flung it at the mirror. Then she threw her chair aside and wiped the message with her hand until the glass was smeared and her hand looked like it was covered with blood.

Terror replaced rage as a shadow suddenly caught her eye.

Janna spun around, her gaze darting to the costume rack on the other side of the dressing room. The costumes hung straight and still. No one crouched behind them. The room was empty.

Cautiously, Janna moved to the open door and peered out into the hallway.

Empty and quiet. Frighteningly quiet.

I'm closer than you think.

Was he waiting for her in another dressing room?

Don't stay down here, she told herself. Go. Run! Get out of this dungeon!

Swallowing hard, Janna took a deep breath and raced for the stairs.

As she put her foot on the first step, a shadow loomed in front of her.

Janna's scream echoed off the cement walls as the shadow closed in.

Chapter 10

"What is the *matter* with you?" Liz cried, staring down at Janna from the step above. "What are you screaming about?"

"I . . . I thought. . ." Janna swallowed hard. "What are you doing here, Liz?"

"Getting my eardrums broken, obviously," Liz snapped. "What kind of question is that? I work here, remember? For your information, Gray asked me to find you."

"Gray?"

"Our choreographer?" Liz said. "The one who happens to be wondering why you're not onstage with the rest of us."

The rehearsal, Janna thought. She was late getting back to it and Gray was probably furious.

Liz spun around and started up the stairs. "Are you coming?" she called back over her shoulder. "Or shall I tell Gray you've totally lost it?"

Her mocking laugh rang in Janna's ears.

I'm closer than you think. We'll be together soon.

Soon. Soon. Soon.

The word echoed like a drumbeat in Janna's mind, blocking out the fifties' beat she was trying to dance to in rehearsal.

It's not over, she thought. It's not over.

He's here.

He knows where I am and he's not giving up.

"Hold it!" Gray Williams called. "Janna!"

Janna's head snapped up as the other dancers shuffled to a stop.

"You're moving like a sleepwalker," Gray told her. "I want to see some spark."

Janna nodded, embarrassed at being singled out.

"Okay, people, let's do it again," Gray said.

As they scrambled into position, Eric patted Janna's shoulder. Gillian and Toni shot her sympathetic glances.

Liz didn't even look at her. Liz's face was a picture of concentration. She must have heard Gray's comment, but she was totally focused on her dancing.

Like I should be, Janna thought.

Like I used to be.

"Janna!" Gray's voice was exasperated. "Is there something that fascinates you about the lighting arrangement?"

Janna shook her head. She'd been staring at the follow spot, remembering.

Not concentrating.

"Then maybe you could take your eyes off it long enough to see where you are," Gray told her.

Janna looked. She was too far stage left. One of the wing curtains was brushing her shoulder.

Concentrate, she told herself. Concentrate!

As she moved into the right position, Eric gave her shoulder another pat. "I tried to warn you," he whispered.

"It's not your fault," Janna whispered back.

It was the stalker's.

But it was hers, too. She was letting him get to her. And she was messing up, big time. Losing it, like Liz said.

You can't let it happen, she told herself. You have to block it out.

As rehearsal continued, Janna tried desperately to concentrate. She'd do fine for five minutes. Then the red words on the mirror would pop into her mind. She'd smell the scent of roses. Hear that voice on the telephone. See those eyes outside her motel room window.

She'd remember Toni's words, *brutally murdered*.

And she'd mess up again.

"All right, people, that's it," Gray finally called out. He sounded disgusted.

Janna put her hands on her hips and stared at the stage floor. She didn't want to meet his eyes.

"Let's get out of here and spend the whole afternoon in the pool," Gillian said as the dancers started to leave the stage.

Janna shook her head. "Eric said he'd stick around and practice with me. We're going to go over the last dance until I get it right."

"Janna, what's wrong?" Toni asked, pushing her red hair out of her eyes and peering at Janna's face.

"The stalker," Janna whispered. "He left me a message on the dressing room mirror. He's here, in Braxton!"

"Jimmy Dare?" Gillian asked.

Slowly, Janna shook her head. "It's not Jimmy. It wasn't his handwriting. He's not the one."

"What?" Toni gasped. "Then who is?"

"I don't know," Janna cried.

Toni gasped. "So that's why you couldn't . . ."

"Dance," Janna finished bitterly. "Right. I couldn't concentrate."

"Well, no wonder!" Toni cried.

Gillian glanced at Gray, who was talking to Vic. "Have you told him about this?"

"What can Gray do?" Janna asked. "I mean, the guy hasn't hurt me. He hasn't even threatened me, not in so many words. And I don't even know who it is! What's Gray supposed to do about some shadow?"

"He's no shadow," Gillian said, blotting her forehead with a towel. "I hate to say it, but just because he hasn't hurt you yet doesn't mean he's not thinking about it."

"I know that!" Janna cried. "And it's making me a nervous wreck. He probably gets some kind of sick thrill out of pulling my strings like this. But I can't let him ruin my dancing. I have to keep working, that's all I can do!"

That was the problem, she thought, as Gillian and Toni left for the dressing room. Unless the stalker showed his face, there was nothing anybody could do.

"And *one* and *two* and *jump*," Eric called out.

Janna stepped and then leaped toward Eric's outstretched arms. But she landed wide of her mark and well out of his reach.

"This is hopeless."

"No it's not. Come on. Try it again," Eric said. "You'll get it."

"It's been an hour and I haven't gotten it yet," Janna sighed. "Thanks for putting up with me, Eric, but I'm afraid I'm wasting your time."

Breathless and disappointed in herself, she sat down on the dark green rug in the lobby of the theater. Gray was working with some of the principals onstage, and the lobby was the only other space big enough to dance in.

"You're having a lousy day, that's all." Eric wiped his face and slung the towel around his neck.

"Yeah." Janna leaned her forehead on her knees.

"Everybody has them, Janna," Eric said. "Listen, I hear your motel has a pool."

"Yes." Janna raised her head. "That's your reward for working overtime with me, Eric.

Let's go on over there and jump in."

"Great. Thanks, Janna. See you there." Eric grabbed his duffel bag and left.

Standing up, Janna bent from the waist and took a couple of deep breaths.

Eric was great to stay, but it hadn't helped. Janna had never danced so badly. Even when she'd had a lousy rehearsal, somehow she'd always managed to come through during performance.

For the first time in her life, she was afraid she wouldn't.

I'm closer than you think.

Janna shuddered. Was it just a sick game? Or did he really have something more in mind?

Like murder?

Blotting her forehead with her arm, Janna crossed to the auditorium doors, eased one open and peeked inside.

The Burger Palace Boys were rehearsing "Greased Lightning."

Janna didn't see Gray, but there were several heads poking up from the front row seats. His was probably one of them.

She eased the door closed. She wasn't going to talk to Gray. Not yet, at least. It wouldn't help.

What would?

Ryan. She'd invite him to the pool. Swimming and Ryan. Maybe the combination would ease her nerves.

Tired and sweaty, Janna went down a side hall that led to the backstage area. She glanced around, then moved toward the stage and scanned the scaffolds above. No Ryan.

Maybe he was downstairs. She had to go get her bag anyway. She'd look for him there.

At the top of the stairs, she hesitated, biting her lip nervously.

Go on, she urged herself. Don't let him do this to you. Don't let him control your life.

Forcing herself to go downstairs, Janna walked along the narrow hall, peering cautiously in each door until she reached her dressing room.

The door stood open. Voices came from inside.

She looked in.

Ryan was there.

Only he wasn't alone. He was with Liz Thompson.

And they weren't talking anymore.

Liz's arms were wrapped around Ryan's neck. Her body was pressed tight against his.

And her lips were locked on his mouth.

Chapter 11

Snapping her fingers, Janna spun toward Eric, leaping up and landing in a split at his feet. She tilted on the landing, but managed not to topple sideways. Her smile felt pasted on. Her legs and arms were like lead. Janna was exhausted.

The curtain swung closed.

"No boos, at least," Eric muttered as he and Janna ran offstage. "I'm surprised they're even clapping."

"They're probably clapping out of sympathy," Janna said. "Or relief."

The performance had been flat as a rug and full of mistakes from beginning to end. Missed cues. Late entrances. A piece of scenery that wobbled so badly it upstaged everybody. Everything seemed to go wrong.

The director wasn't in town yet, so Vic was

in charge. He'd given everybody a pep talk during intermission, trying to get some spark into them. He'd been cheerful then.

Now, as Janna dashed past him, he just looked mad.

"Watch out for Gray," Gillian murmured, standing next to Janna and smoothing down the skirt of her costume. "He's on the war-path. We were *so* bad!"

At least he's not mad at just me, Janna thought grimly, taking her place for the curtain call. She wasn't the only one who'd messed up tonight.

But the thought didn't really help.

The curtain opened. Eric grabbed her hand and they ran onstage. The band played a re-prise from *We Go Together*.

Not Ryan and I, Janna thought. We defi-nitely don't go together.

Why had she let herself fall for him like that? After Jimmy, she should have been completely on guard. Instead, she'd actually thought there was something special happening between her and Ryan.

Liz had warned her, of course. Now she knew the reason — Liz was jealous, just as she was jealous of Janna's dancing. Liz wanted Ryan back.

Well, she could have him.

The curtain closed and Eric squeezed her hand. "What do you want to bet they'll open the curtain again and the place'll be empty?"

Janna sighed. "Either that or they'll stay and throw tomatoes."

When the curtain opened, the audience was still there. Still clapping. No tomatoes.

But only two curtain calls.

The cast scattered as quickly as possible. Everybody knew they'd done badly. Tomorrow, they'd get up there and do it again, better.

Will I be any better? Janna wondered, pulling the ribbon from her ponytail and shaking her hair loose.

Grateful that there wasn't going to be a cast call so Vic could chew them out, Janna hurried through the wings toward the stairs.

Ryan, rushing past with a hammer, stopped when he saw her. "Gotta fix that flat," he said, flashing her a dimpled smile. "Why don't you stick around and we can grab a bite after I'm through?"

Why don't you just stick it? Janna thought.

"Sorry. No," she said.

"No? That's it?"

"That's it," she told him. She started to leave, but Ryan took her arm.

"What's going on?" he asked.

Janna sighed. "Look, Ryan, I've got a lot on my mind, okay? Gray's on my case, and I want to get a good night's sleep so I can do a decent job tomorrow."

He shook his head. "That doesn't explain why you've all of a sudden turned into an iceberg."

He hadn't seen her outside the dressing room, Janna reminded herself. Obviously. He hadn't seen her because he'd been too busy with Liz.

"Ryan, I saw you in the dressing room," she told him. "You and Liz."

Ryan's eyes widened and a slow blush crept up his neck. He started to reply, but a crew member rushed up and grabbed his arm. "Vic's out for blood, Mitchell," Jake muttered. "Get a move on."

As Jake pulled him away, Ryan glanced back. His gold-flecked eyes were hot with anger. "This isn't the end of it, Janna!" he called over his shoulder.

Janna didn't answer. It *was* the end. It had to be.

On top of everything else, she didn't need Mr. Heartbreaker in her life.

"Well, of course he was mad, Janna," Toni said the next morning. She pulled the straps of her pink bikini down and rubbed more sunscreen on her freckled shoulders. "You didn't give him a chance to explain."

"Too bad Liz went shopping," Gillian remarked, floating on her back in the motel swimming pool. "We could dunk her until she promised to stay away from Ryan."

"Let's not talk about Ryan anymore. Or Liz." Janna sat on the tiled edge of the pool, her feet dangling in the cool water. Maybe if they didn't talk about Ryan, she could forget about him.

Not likely. Seeing Ryan and Liz stuck together like they were glued had made her furious. But it also hurt. A lot. She'd even dreamed about it and waked up with tears on her face.

Sighing, Janna pulled up the loose strap of her green, one-piece suit and stared out at the road. A white car drove slowly by the motel. Her gaze followed it for a moment, then she looked back at her roommates. "Has anybody seen Bearyshnikov?" she asked. "I looked everywhere for him last night, and this morning, and I couldn't find him."

Gillian sat up and began treading water. "Maybe you left him back in Glenwood Junction."

Janna shook her head. "I'm positive I brought him."

"He'll turn up," Toni said.

He'd better, Janna thought. That stuffed bear was her good-luck charm. And the way things were going, she needed all the luck she could get.

"Come on in the pool, you guys," Gillian urged, splashing water on the other two. "We actually have it to ourselves and you're just sitting there."

Toni put down her paperback and jumped in. Janna stood up and walked around to the diving board. Standing on the end of it, she bounced a couple of times, then raised her arms.

A white car drove slowly down the road.

The same white car she saw driving by the motel.

It's him, she thought with a shiver. He's here, right now.

In a panic, Janna jumped in feet first. "He's here!" she cried, swimming furiously underneath the diving board. "The stalker's here! He's driven by twice already in a white car!"

Gillian and Toni scrambled out of the pool and looked around. "There's no white car there now," Toni said, shading her eyes against the sun. "He must be gone."

"Are you sure it was the same car both times?" Gillian asked.

Janna nodded, still beneath the diving board. Her teeth were chattering.

"Calm down, Janna!" Toni urged. "You've got to calm down. Maybe it wasn't the stalker. It could have been just some guy who saw three gorgeous girls in sexy swimsuits and decided to cruise by for a second look."

Janna climbed out of the pool and sluiced water off her face. Toni could be right, she told herself as she climbed onto the board again. You're freaking out. Jumping at anything that looks suspicious.

Don't let him control you!

As she climbed out of the pool, she glanced toward the road.

The white car moved slowly by the motel, one more time.

* * *

Half an hour later, Janna left the motel and headed for the theater. She needed to dance. To practice. To try to forget Ryan and the stalker.

As she started down the road, her eyes darted nervously back and forth. That tall, stooped man by the phone booth. Was that the stalker?

Or was that him up ahead, the heavyset, bearded guy coming out of the 7-Eleven?

Or was he in his white car, waiting for her around the corner?

Nervously, Janna hitched her duffel bag higher on her shoulder and picked up her pace. By the time she reached the drive leading to the theater, she was running.

Quickly, she went around back and pulled open a stage door. The backstage was dark. The entire theater was dark.

"Anybody here?" Janna called out. No answer. Rehearsal was over two hours away and the theater was empty.

Janna hurried through the wings and flipped on some stage lights, illuminating the Burger Palace set. The crew must have worked on it all night, Janna thought.

She dropped her bag and slipped out of her wraparound denim skirt. Underneath she wore a dark blue body suit. She pulled on some leg warmers and a pair of ballet slippers, then walked to center stage.

As she began some leg stretches, Janna felt that familiar fear wash over her again. Was the stalker near? Watching her?

She peered into the empty auditorium. Up to the catwalk. At the scaffolding above her.

No one.

Stop thinking about him, Janna told herself. Stop thinking about the stalker, and Ryan. Just dance.

Janna took the hand of her imaginary partner and began her routine.

"And *one* and *two* and *three* and *four*. No!" She came to an abrupt stop. "On the downbeat, Janna," she lectured herself. "The *down*beat."

Back to first position. "*And* one *and* two *and* three *and* four." Janna began again. Better, she thought, but still not good enough.

Do it again.

She counted the beats in her head, then stopped.

Were those footsteps she heard?

She looked around again. Didn't see anyone.

She waited, listening.

The theater was quiet.

Too quiet.

Get out of here, Janna told herself. Remember what happened the last time you were alone on an empty stage.

Shuddering at the memory of that single rose falling toward her from the catwalk, she turned to leave.

Had she heard something again? A quiet rustle from behind the set?

Janna spun around. She was almost center stage, directly in front of the doors of the Burger Palace. Wood on the bottom. On top, sheets of milky plastic, stretched tightly to look like glass.

Was that a shadow behind them?

Janna's heart knocked against her chest. She started to move again.

Suddenly, a loud creaking sound split the air.

Janna gasped. The whole set was falling toward her. She started to scream. Took one running step.

And then the pain exploded in her head.

She felt her knees buckle, felt her body falling.

Saw the dusty stage floor rise up toward her face.

And then her world went black.

Chapter 12

"Janna?" a voice murmured. Then more loudly, "Janna!"

"Look at all the blood!" another voice said. "Is she okay?"

"Janna?" the first voice said again. "Janna."

Janna's head pounded like a jackhammer. She tried to say something, but all that came out was a groan.

"Come on, Janna, open your eyes." A third voice. Urgent. Worried.

Ryan's voice.

Janna forced her eyes open. Everything was blurry. And her head! What had happened to her head? It hurt so much she felt like throwing up.

Janna blinked, and Ryan's face came into focus.

She groaned again and let her eyes shut. Heard shuffling. A flurry of whispers. Felt something soft press down above her right eye.

The pain was incredible. She cried out.

"Sorry, but you've got a nasty cut," a voice she finally identified as Vic's told her. "Gotta press this gauze on there to stop the bleeding."

The bleeding. Blood. *Look at all the blood*, someone had said. Panicked, Janna tried to get up.

A wave of dizziness washed over her and she began to fall again. Hands steadied her. Gray's. Vic's. Ryan's.

"Take it easy, Janna," Gray said as they helped her to sit. He took her hand and pressed it over the gauze. "Hold that in place and rest a few minutes."

Almost immediately, the blood seeped through the gauze and onto Janna's fingers. She shuddered. Vic took the sopping cloth from her and gave her another piece.

"I think it's slowing down," Vic said. "Give it another minute. Good thing the set missed your eye."

"The set?" Janna glanced around.

The entire back wall of the Burger Palace was down. Canvas torn. Plastic ripped. Wood frames broken and splintered.

"What happened?" Janna asked. "It was up before. I was dancing and . . ." she paused, remembering.

The footsteps. The shadow.

Had she imagined them or had they really been there?

Janna glanced at Ryan.

"You were dancing and what?" Vic asked.

"And it fell," Janna said slowly, still looking at Ryan.

Ryan's lean face tightened. "I'm sorry," he said softly. "We worked on it half the night. I thought it was secure. I'm really sorry, Janna."

"The bleeding's just about stopped," Vic said, relieved. He cleaned the cut and put a bandage on it. "But you ought to see a doctor."

"No!" Janna cried out. "I don't want that. You said the bleeding's stopped. I just need to rest awhile."

Vic frowned, but didn't argue. "Okay, then somebody'll drive you back to your motel."

"I will," Ryan said quickly.

Janna didn't want Ryan. She shook her head. The throbbing got worse.

"I need you here, Ryan," Vic told him. "We've got a major repair job on our hands. Get Jake to take her."

Vic and Gray helped Janna to her feet. Her knees wobbled, but she managed to stay up.

She had to stay up. She had to dance tonight!

She started to walk. Her head banged with each step. "Not so fast," Gray said, putting his arm around her waist. "Listen, Janna, you've got the rest of the day off, and I'm taking you out of the show tonight."

"No!" Janna protested.

"Look at you," he told her. "You've got a bad cut and you can hardly walk. You're in no shape to dance."

"Not now, maybe, but I will be later."

Gray shook his head. "Don't argue," he said, as Janna started to protest again. "I should send you to the hospital for X rays."

"I don't want to go to the hospital!" Janna said.

"Fine, but you're still not dancing tonight," Gray told her. "That's an order."

"But I'll be back onstage tomorrow, right?" Janna said.

Gray frowned. "We'll see."

As Jake took Janna's arm and started to help

her offstage, she turned back to Gray. "Who'll take my place tonight?"

"Liz Thompson," he told her.

Janna's head began throbbing worse than before.

Liz took Ryan.

And now she'd taken Janna's dance.

Thunder rumbled in the distance as Janna stuck her key in the motel room door. Clouds covered the sky and the air was thick and hot.

Dropping her bag, Janna shut the door behind her and leaned against it, taking a deep breath.

Her head still throbbed. She ached all over.

Aspirin. Aspirin and maybe a hot shower.

Walking unsteadily, Janna went into the bathroom and found the bottle of aspirin. As she swallowed two of the pills, she stared at her reflection in the mirror.

Pale. Blood matted with dirt in her tangled dark hair.

And fear in her eyes.

What if she hadn't imagined the footsteps?

If she hadn't, then someone had pushed the entire set down on her.

I'm closer than you think.

Janna finished the glass of water, then went

back into the main room. She was too tired to shower.

All she wanted was to put her head down and sleep away the ache and the fear.

The room was icy. She turned the air conditioner down a notch. She peeled off the filthy bodysuit and pulled jeans and a dark-red sweatshirt on against the chill.

Pictures flashed behind her closed eyes as she lay on her back across one of the beds. The shadow backstage. The set, falling as if in slow motion. The circle of worried faces looking down at her when she came to.

Janna rolled onto her side. Soon she felt herself sink deeper into the mattress. Felt the banging in her head start to ease. The pictures stopped flashing, and she fell into a deep sleep.

She was back onstage, trying to dance. . . .

It was very important. If she didn't dance well, Gray was going to make her take lessons from Liz Thompson. "Liz is the best," he said, as Janna stumbled around. "Liz can teach you a thing or two."

"No." Janna tried to yell, but her voice was weak.

"Dance, Janna!" Gray cried. His face loomed at her from the darkness of the wings. "Dance!"

Janna took a deep breath. Smiled out at the

empty auditorium. Started to lift a foot.

And fell hard onto the stage.

"No, no, no!" Gray shrieked. "You're out, Janna! You're out of the show!"

"Give me another chance," Janna begged. "Please!"

She scrambled to her feet. She'd been dancing almost all her life. She could do this, she knew she could.

"One, two, three, four," she counted. She lifted her foot again, raised her arms.

Something jerked at her, pulling her sideways. She stumbled, almost fell again.

Why couldn't she dance? What was stopping her?

Gray was still yelling at her from the wings. Janna started to panic, her breath coming in ragged gasps. What was wrong with her? Why couldn't she dance?

Suddenly, her right arm jerked up. Then her left leg. Then her other arm.

Janna tugged, tried to dance, but it was impossible. Something was pulling at her, making her move like a crazy puppet.

A puppet! A puppet on strings!

Janna looked up. Peering down at her from the lights above the stage was Liz Thompson.

Her icy eyes were full of scorn. Her red mouth was a sneer.

In one of her hands was a bunch of strings extending down to Janna, attached to her hands, feet, and head. With a sneer, Liz jerked on them.

Janna's feet flew out from under her.

"You're losing it, Janna!" Liz called down, laughing. "You're definitely losing it!"

Turning and twisting, Janna tried to break the strings, but she just got more and more entangled. "Stop!" she cried. "Stop jerking me around!"

She looked up again. Liz was still there. But she wasn't alone anymore.

Ryan was with her. Now Ryan was pulling the strings, making Janna stumble. The gold flecks in his eyes glittered when she fell.

Suddenly Jimmy Dare's face appeared next to Ryan's. "You're mine, Janna!" Jimmy shouted. "You belong with me!"

Jimmy grabbed the strings and yanked.

Janna felt herself rising from the stage floor. "Get a life, Jimmy!" she cried up at him. "Stop trying to control mine!"

A fourth face appeared then, but it stayed hidden in the shadows so Janna couldn't make it out. "You're the most beautiful dancer I ever saw, Janna!" a voice called down to her. "I love you. I love you to death!"

Janna hit the floor with a thump, then felt herself jerked to her feet and bounced from one side of the stage to the other.

As she looked up, desperately trying to keep her footing, Janna saw that all of them were pulling the strings now.

All of them were controlling her.

"You're out!" Gray shrieked again. "You're out of the show! You can't dance at all!"

"It's not me," Janna cried. "It's them. They're controlling me. Let me get free and I'll show you I can dance."

Back and forth, upstage and downstage. Janna felt herself flying. Her feet barely touched the ground. Her head was ringing.

"No more," she cried. "No more!"

Janna jerked awake, her heart pounding. She felt the sweat pouring off her face. Heard the steady drone of the air conditioner.

A nightmare. She'd had a horrible nightmare.

Part of it was still with her. The ringing. The ringing in her head.

No, not in her head. It was the telephone.

Groggy and dizzy, Janna glanced at the clock as she reached for the phone. She'd been asleep for more than six hours. "Hello," she murmured.

"Janna."

Just the one word, breathed like a sigh.

"Yes?" Janna's hand tightened around the phone. "Who is this?"

"You know."

The voice was muffled. Soft. Was it the same voice that had called her before?

Janna started to speak, but the caller interrupted her. "Did you have a good nap, Janna? I hope so. Because you're going to need your strength." The voice changed. Still soft, but cold. So cold. "By the way, blood-red's the perfect color for you. Someday soon, you're going to be covered in the real thing."

Janna's heart seemed to stop. But her mind began racing.

The sweatshirt. The dark red sweatshirt she'd put on before she fell asleep.

No one else knew she had it on. No one but her caller.

No one but her caller knew she'd been asleep.

He can see me, Janna thought. He's looking at me, right now!

Slowly, Janna turned her head toward the window.

Chapter 13

Rain. Sheets of it, blowing sideways in the wind. Slanting down on the deserted road.

The road was dark except for a high, arcing street lamp. Its light was a misty orange halo, shining weakly onto a telephone booth only forty feet away from Janna's motel room.

The phone booth was occupied.

Janna saw a pale smudge that might have been a hand or a face. Except for that, all she could see was the dark shadowy outline of a figure.

But she knew.

She knew it was the stalker, watching her through the rain.

Taunting her.

Threatening her.

Janna was terrified. But her head was clear now. And the nightmare of being pulled back and forth like a helpless, mindless puppet made her realize that that was exactly how she'd been acting. Helpless. Mindless.

No more, she thought. Not anymore.

A wave of anger surged inside her, wiping out the terror. "Listen!" she hissed into the phone. "You want to keep playing this game? Fine. But guess what? I'm about to even the score!"

She slammed the phone down, then pulled it off the table and onto the floor. On her knees, out of the stalker's sight now, she punched in the number for the police.

"Somebody's across the street from my motel room, in a phone booth!" she cried as soon as she was connected. "He called and he knew what I . . ."

"Calm down, please, and give me your name and number," a woman's voice said.

"Janna Richards," Janna said quickly. "I don't know the number. The . . . I can't remember the name! It's a motel someplace outside of town!"

"All right, ma'am, and this person is where?"

"I told you," Janna said urgently. "In a phone booth across the street. He's been watching me."

"Do you know who it is? Can you see him now?"

"I don't want to look — he'll see and figure out I'm calling you!" Janna said impatiently. "I want you to come arrest him!"

"Try to calm down," the woman repeated.

Janna clenched her teeth. "I'm telling you he's out there right now and I want you to do something about it."

"Yes, ma'am, I understand that, but I need to . . ."

"There isn't time for twenty questions!" Janna shouted. She started to say more, then changed her mind and hung up.

No time to waste. No time to wait. If the police couldn't do something, then she would.

She wasn't about to let him get away!

Crossing the room in three steps, she flung open the door and raced outside.

Windblown rain slammed against her like a wall, tried to push her back. Janna leaned into it, peeled a strand of hair out of her eyes, and kept running.

Past the swimming pool, across the parking lot. Rain like bullets on her head, her back.

Don't let him get away!

Onto a narrow strip of grass. Swampy now. Mud oozing between her bare toes.

Take him by surprise. Beat him at his own sick game!

Over the slippery curb and into the street. Water flowed down it in a torrent, foaming around her ankles.

Breathless and furious, Janna raced up to the telephone booth.

Empty.

No one in sight. No cars. No figure, slinking away in the darkness.

Drenched to the skin, Janna approached the booth and looked inside.

The receiver was off the hook, hanging from its silvery, snakelike cord.

Slowly, she reached out and picked up the receiver.

He held this in his hand. His lips touched it. His breath made it warm.

With a shudder, she dropped the phone.

Next time, she thought. I'll get him next time.

Flinging her sopping hair from her face, Janna started back across the street. She looked both ways, wondering if she'd see a white car speeding off from somewhere nearby. But the street remained deserted.

Rain slanted into her eyes, and Janna put her head down as she walked into the wind.

The cut above her eye stung and her head was throbbing again. She felt cold, inside and out. As she walked along the edge of the pool, she crossed her arms and stuck her hands way up inside the sleeves of her sweatshirt.

A noise brought her head up.

Too late.

A powerful blow to the back knocked the breath out of her and threw her completely off her feet.

Stunned, Janna tried to free her hands for balance, but she couldn't get them out of the sleeves in time.

She was falling with no way to stop herself. Falling headfirst into the deep end of the swimming pool.

She opened her mouth for air but water filled it, seeping down her throat and into her lungs.

Her jeans, heavy with water, dragged at her legs. Pulled her farther and farther below the surface.

Panicked and choking, Janna struggled desperately to free her hands as she sank to the bottom of the pool.

Chapter 14

She couldn't breathe!

She had to breathe, had to cough the water out of her lungs, but there was no air!

Totally disoriented, Janna couldn't tell which way was up. She felt herself rolling over and tried to kick with her legs. Her chin bumped hard on the rough bottom of the pool. The jarring impact shot such a wave of pain through her head, she instinctively opened her mouth to cry out.

Tiny pinpoints of light danced in front of her eyes. Her lungs were on fire, begging for air.

She was going to drown!

Her stomach muscles cramped with the urge to choke out the water she'd already inhaled.

Don't do it! Don't cough, don't try to breathe!

Get your hands free!

With the blood pounding in her head and her whole body screaming for air, Janna finally pulled one of her hands out of the sleeve of her heavy, wet sweatshirt.

Her feet grazed the bottom of the pool, and she used the last bit of strength in her legs to push off. Her other hand came free and she shot upward, her body cutting through the water like a rocket.

At last she broke the surface, sucking in the air in huge, heaving gasps. She grasped the edge of the pool with one hand, then the other. Her arms quivered as she tried to pull herself out.

Halfway was as far as she could go. With her legs still in the water, she lay across the wet tiles surrounding the pool, shuddering and choking.

Got to get out, she told herself. Got to get inside.

And then she heard footsteps coming toward the pool. Slapping on the wet tiles.

Coming closer.

"No!" she screamed, raising her head.

Gillian and Toni were running toward her.

Relief flooded through her, and Janna began to drag her legs up. Her roommates grabbed her arms and pulled, and at last she was out of the pool.

"What happened?" Toni cried, her blue eyes shocked and worried. "You look half-drowned! What happened to you?"

Janna's whole body shuddered as she choked out the words. "The stalker," she cried hoarsely. "The stalker!"

"Are you going to be all right now?" the policeman asked.

Janna nodded, too stunned and tired to say anything. She huddled on one of the beds with dry clothes on and two blankets around her.

But she still couldn't get warm.

"Are you sure there's nothing you can do?" Gillian asked him again.

The policeman sighed sympathetically. He was at the door, on his way out. He'd come quickly when Gillian called, but after a few minutes of talking to him, telling him what had happened, Janna realized he was right — he couldn't do much of anything.

"Like I said," the policeman repeated, "if we knew who we were up against, we could slap a restraining order on him. But without any ID, we're in the dark."

In the dark, Janna thought. Like me.

She reached for the cup of hot tea Toni had made. Her hand shook, but she managed a sip.

"Miss Richards?"

Janna glanced up. The policeman looked concerned.

"Remember what I told you," he said. "Start keeping a log. If this person calls again, write it down. The time. What he says. There's always a chance he'll slip up and say something that identifies him. And if you get any more notes, be sure to hang on to them."

Janna nodded again.

"And call us immediately if you *do* hear from him," the policeman reminded her.

"I will. Thanks," Janna said.

With a concerned smile, the officer said good night and left the motel room.

"Can you believe that?" Gillian asked, shutting the door. "Somebody calls and threatens Janna and then almost drowns her and nobody can do anything!"

"It's really lousy," Toni agreed. "But you can't blame the police, I guess. After all, he's right — how can they stop this guy if they don't know who he is?"

Janna finished the tea and pulled the blankets tighter around her.

"You okay, Janna?" Toni asked. "Want some more tea?"

"No thanks."

Gillian frowned at her. "I hate to say this after what happened, Janna. But running out to that phone booth was a totally insane thing to do."

"Maybe so," Janna said. "But I was so furious. Catching him was the only thing on my mind. It still is."

Gillian eyed her skeptically. "You're kidding, right?"

"No, I'm insane, remember?" Janna cried, suddenly angry.

"Sorry," Gillian said quickly. "I didn't mean it that way."

"I know." Janna sighed, frustrated. "I'm not mad at you, Gill. I'm mad at the stalker. Look at me! I'm sitting here like some kind of invalid, drinking hot tea and shivering under the covers! And I don't know who to blame for it!"

"Well, that's not your fault," Toni pointed out. "I mean, the creep hasn't shown his face. You can't fight a shadow, like you said. How are you supposed to know who it is? It could be anyone. It could even be someone in the company."

Toni's eyes widened as soon as she realized what she'd said.

But the words were out. She couldn't take them back.

Janna was still thinking about it when the door opened and Liz walked into the room.

Liz shut the door and leaned against it, kicking off her wet shoes and complaining about the rain.

Janna and the others watched her silently.

Finally Liz glanced up. "What's going on? What's everybody staring at?"

"You," Gillian said sharply. "Where've you been all this time, Liz?"

"Where have I been?" Liz's eyes narrowed and her voice was cold. "Where I've been is no one's business but mine. Got that?"

"You saw her race out before curtain calls were even over, Toni," Gillian said at the theater the next night. "She had plenty of time to get back to the motel before we did."

"Maybe," Toni said. "And I know she's jealous and everything, but I really can't believe she's the one trying to hurt Janna."

Janna smiled grimly. "The important thing is I'm dancing tonight. No matter what Liz or anybody does. And I'm going to keep dancing."

She and Toni and Gillian were in the green room, a room offstage where actors could wait until they had to be on. A battered couch and three lumpy, overstuffed chairs lined the walls. Weeks-old magazines were scattered on two rickety tables. A coffeemaker and Styrofoam cups stood on a third.

Janna checked the wall clock. Twenty-five minutes until the final number. She smiled again. *She* was dancing it tonight, not Liz. She was back where she belonged.

And she was going to stay there.

As Gillian started to say something, Ryan stuck his head in the door. "Janna? Could I talk to you for a minute?"

Janna looked at the wall clock again. She didn't want to talk, but maybe she should just get it over with.

"Come on in, Ryan," Toni said, leaping off the chair. She nudged Gillian in the shoulder. "We were just leaving."

Ryan waited until Gillian and Toni were gone. Then he turned to Janna. "First — how's your head?" he asked.

"Hard," Janna replied. "It's fine, Ryan."

"Good." He took a deep breath. "Okay. You said you saw me and Liz."

"I did," Janna said, standing up. "I got hit on

the head *after* that, so I'm sure I wasn't seeing things."

"Whoa." Ryan held up his hand. "I'm not accusing you of seeing things. You saw what you saw, okay? But you didn't give me a chance to explain."

"I know I didn't," Janna told him. "But I'm listening now."

"Right. Liz came on to me, Janna," Ryan said. "I was walking past the dressing room, she called me inside, asked me about some prop, and the next thing I knew she was all over me."

Janna didn't say anything.

"Talk about a major shock," Ryan said, shaking his head. "I mean, Liz and I dated a few times last summer, but it didn't work out, so . . ."

"Yeah, she said you dropped her for somebody else," Janna told him.

Ryan barked out a laugh. "I didn't 'drop' her, Janna. I told her as nicely as possible that she wasn't my type. She was insulted in a major way, treated me like I was invisible after that. That's why her come-on yesterday freaked me out."

Janna stared at him, wanting to believe him.

"Anyway, after I managed to peel her off

me, I told her I wasn't interested," Ryan said. "But I guess you didn't stay to hear that."

"No. I didn't," Janna said. She sighed. "Look, Ryan . . ."

"There's no way I can prove it to you," Ryan said, "but it's the truth."

"Maybe it is," Janna said. "But Ryan, listen. I'm tired of people jerking me around. It started to ruin my dancing and I'm not going to let it happen anymore."

"I'm not jerking you around, Janna," Ryan said angrily.

"Then give me some room, okay?" Janna asked. "That's what I want. I want you to back off and give me some room!"

Janna's eyes suddenly filled with tears. Before they spilled over, she rushed past Ryan and out the green room door.

As the curtain closed on the final number, Janna and Eric ran breathlessly offstage.

Gray stood in the wings, a rare smile on his face. "Nice work, Janna," he said, patting her on the shoulder. "I was worried after yesterday, but you came back stronger than ever."

"Thanks, Gray," Janna laughed, exhilarated. She'd done it. She'd danced the way she knew she could.

And she'd keep dancing like this from now on, no matter what happened.

No matter who or what tried to keep her down.

Still holding Eric's hand, she spun around and ran back onstage for curtain calls.

The audience was on its feet, clapping in cadence. Janna flashed a brilliant smile as the dancers stood in line to bow.

"Great show, Janna," Eric said. "I knew you could do it."

"I had a great partner," she told him.

Eric grinned and turned to Liz, who stood next to him. "Can you believe the way Janna danced after what happened to her yesterday?" he asked.

The curtain closed and Liz dropped her pasted-on smile. "Actually, no," she snapped, looking like she'd bitten into a lemon. "I was sure Gray would give her at least a couple of days off to recuperate. She could use it with everything that's been happening to her lately."

The curtain opened, and Janna smiled out at the audience. A couple of days? she thought. Liz would like to see me take a whole month off. "Thanks for your concern, Liz," she said through her smile. "But I'm fine now."

The applause swelled. Janna bowed and straightened up.

Just before the curtain closed, she saw him.

He was in the second row center, standing. Clapping.

Watching her. *Her*, and nobody else.

His eyes didn't leave her face.

His hungry blue eyes.

Chapter 15

Stan, Janna thought as the curtain closed for the last time.

Her stammering, blushing, blue-eyed fan.

Janna dropped Eric's hand and pushed her way offstage into the wings.

Stan's shy act was just a fake. Stan had followed her here. It was him, all the time.

I'm closer than you think, he'd written on the mirror.

And *I'm* closer, too, Stan, Janna thought. Much closer.

You're in for a surprise, Stan.

Because *I'm* going to get *you*!

Past the laughing faces of cast members, Janna hurried through the wings. Pushed through a door that opened onto a side hall. Still in her bobby socks and pink-and-green plaid fifties dress with the puffy crinoline, she ran down the hall toward the lobby.

Audience members were spilling out of the auditorium doors, and the lobby was packed. The people milled about happily, greeting each other and chatting about the show.

Janna stopped at the edge of the crowd.

What color was Stan's hair? Brown, like his girlfriend's. And he was tall. Taller than average. Janna ought to be able to spot him.

She craned her neck, her gaze roving swiftly over male heads. Blond. Reddish. Black. A dozen shades of brown.

No Stan.

Had the coward left already?

There! Way across the lobby, near the outside doors. A tall guy, his back to her. Light brown hair. Thin neck. Yellow collar.

Janna plunged into the crowd. "Excuse me. Excuse me, please!"

Faces turned toward her. Startled at first, annoyed as she pushed her way through. Then smiling when they noticed her costume and makeup.

"Great show," someone said.

"Thanks," Janna murmured automatically. She didn't stop. She couldn't lose him now. "Excuse me," she said again. "Coming through!"

He was still there. His back was still turned, but she could see more of him. A yellow sport shirt, jeans. Tall. Brown-haired. Hands in his pockets.

He looked young from the back. And he seemed to be alone, staring at the framed *Grease* poster just inside the door.

Got you, Stan, Janna thought. Got you now.

A couple of more steps and she was there. Right behind him. She grabbed his arm. "What are you trying to do to me?" she screamed loudly. "Get out of here! Just get out of my life!"

Janna spun him around to face her.

And found herself looking into the startled gray eyes of a total stranger.

"Whoa!" The young man pulled his arm free and backed up a step. "Are you crazy or something?"

"I . . ." Janna stammered. "I . . . I'm sorry. I thought you were someone else."

"Yeah, well, if you ever find the guy, tell him he has my sympathy." Shooting her an angry look, the man left the theater.

Janna turned around and faced a thousand eyes, all shocked. All staring at her like she *was* crazy.

The lobby was totally silent.

Then someone coughed. Someone else laughed a little too loudly. Finally, people started talking again.

Her face flushed with embarrassment, Janna made her way back through the crowd.

"Janna!" someone called sharply.

She glanced at the auditorium door.

Gray stood there, his face like a thundercloud as she walked over to him.

"I'm sorry, Gray," she murmured.

"You should be," he said through clenched teeth. "I know you've been having a rough time, Janna. But my first concern has to be for the whole company. Don't ever let anything like this happen again!"

"I couldn't help it!" Janna cried later, hunching forward in the booth of the coffee shop. "I saw Stan out there! And all I could think of was how he's destroying my life! I had to get him!"

Gillian pushed up the sleeves of her yellow blouse and reached for the ketchup. "I know, but it's dangerous, Janna. Look what happened last night."

"But this was in the lobby," Janna argued. "He couldn't have hurt me there!"

"Yeah, except it wasn't Stan," Toni pointed

out. "Call that police officer and let him handle it."

"All I can tell him is the guy's first name," Janna reminded her. "And that he has brown hair and blue eyes. That doesn't exactly narrow it down."

Gillian thumped ketchup onto her hamburger, then handed the bottle to Janna. "Well, just be careful, okay? And don't do anything to get Gray on your case again."

"All I know is I'm not going to let anyone turn me into a wimp again," Janna declared, pouring ketchup on her fries. "If it means running into the lobby and making a fool of myself, then I'll do it."

Janna bit into a fry and dripped ketchup down the front of her orange T-shirt. She was wiping it with a napkin when a shadow fell across the table.

It was Liz.

"Hi, guys," Liz said. "Mind if I join you?" Without waiting for an answer, she slid into the booth next to Toni.

Gillian and Toni exchanged glances with Janna. Janna shrugged and reached for another fry.

"I wish I could eat things like that," Toni

sighed, breaking the silence. "I always have to watch my weight."

"Some people get all the breaks," Liz commented, pushing her hair back. "Right, Janna?"

Janna bit into the fry.

"So what are you doing here?" Liz asked her. "Not out with Ryan tonight?"

Toni's eyes widened. "That's a cheap shot."

Liz stared at her. "What are you talking about?"

"Oh, come on, Liz," Gillian said. "Janna saw you and Ryan in the dressing room in a major lip-lock, that's what she's talking about."

Liz glanced at Gillian, then at Janna. Her face was flushed, but Janna didn't think she was ashamed.

"How come *you're* not out with Ryan?" Toni asked. "After all, you got him back, right?"

"Yeah, is that where you were last night, by the way?" Gillian asked.

"You are so wrong," Liz said, her eyes flashing. "You are all so totally wrong, I can't believe it."

No one spoke.

"I love the way you just jump to conclusions," Liz said sarcastically. "How about giving me a chance to tell what really happened?"

"Go ahead," Janna told her, eating another french fry. "Let's hear the story."

"It's not a story!" Liz snapped. "It happens to be the truth."

"Let me guess," Gillian said. "Ryan came on to *you*, right?"

"Yes!"

Toni raised her eyebrows.

"That's exactly what happened," Liz continued. "I was in the dressing room and he came in and started talking about what a great time we had last summer. How he kept thinking about me. He even used the same line he used with that rose he gave you, Janna. He said, 'I can't get you out of my mind.'"

"Very good, Liz," Gillian remarked. "You think fast, don't you?"

Liz glared at her.

"Go on, Liz," Toni urged. "Tell us the rest."

"Why should I bother?" Liz said angrily. She started to scoot out of the booth, then stopped and looked at Janna. "I warned you, remember? I told you what Ryan Mitchell was like. But you ignored me. Well, I don't care how mad you are, I'm going to warn you again."

Liz leaned across the table, her face only a foot from Janna's. "Watch out for him," she said. "He practically jumped me in that empty dressing room. He's capable of anything."

Janna frowned. "What do you mean?"

"Remember the set that fell?" Liz said. "Your little swim in the pool last night? And one more thing — that actress Toni told you about. Kathy Kramer, the one who was murdered. She was in *this* company before she went to New York, remember?"

Janna nodded.

"Well, so was Ryan Mitchell," Liz informed her. "A pretty big coincidence if you ask me. Don't be surprised if he's the one who's been stalking you, Janna. You don't have to believe me, but if I were you, I'd be very, very careful. Or it could be your funeral!"

Chapter 16

Janna checked her watch. Almost an hour before she had to be at the theater to get ready for tonight's performance.

She moved along the sidewalk in the small downtown area of Braxton, looking in store windows. Not many stores to choose from. Maybe tomorrow she'd take a bus to a mall for some serious shopping.

A display of running shoes finally caught her eye and she glanced down at her own sneakers. They were practically falling apart, didn't even qualify as grunge anymore.

Pushing open the shop door, Janna went in and picked two pairs to try on. As she laced up the pair with the violet swoosh on the sides, she thought about what Liz had said.

She thought about Ryan Mitchell.

Actually, she hadn't stopped thinking about him.

Ryan was in the dance company with the girl who'd been murdered. Did he know her? Had he stalked her?

No. Stan's in town. You saw him.

Liz is just trying to pull your strings. Don't let her do it.

"Found a pair you like?" the shoe clerk asked, breaking into Janna's thoughts.

Janna stood up and walked around. Perfect. Like walking on air. She charged them, asked the clerk to toss her old ones, and wore the new ones out of the store.

There was still time to walk around some more, but Janna decided to go straight to the theater. Two or three blocks over, then about half a mile up the road. The walk would break in her new shoes.

A white car pulled up to the stop sign at the end of the block.

A white car.

Janna stopped walking.

Who was in that car?

She was facing the passenger side. Couldn't see the driver because of the mix of sun and shade through the overhanging tree branches.

It doesn't have to be the stalker, she told herself. There are a zillion white cars in this world.

Slowly, the car pulled through the intersection. It didn't turn. It moved straight by and out of sight.

But it might have pulled over at the curb, Janna thought. It could be just around the corner. Motor idling. Waiting for her.

She let her breath out. Licked her dry lips. Glanced around.

On her right, an alleyway. Wooden fences with garbage cans leaning against them. The alley led clear through to the next street. She saw two cars passing by.

Neither of them was white.

Quickly, Janna ducked into the alley.

She walked briskly, swinging her dance bag by the straps. Kept her eyes on the patch of street ahead. A blue car drove by. A brown one.

She glanced over her shoulder. No one coming.

Janna was starting to relax when a loud crash sounded just behind her.

She jumped a mile and whirled around, her heart racing.

A metal garbage can lay on its side, rocking back and forth. Its lid was off, a green plastic trash bag spilling out.

A yellow cat crept from behind the can. It stopped and glared when it saw Janna, then streaked across the alley, through a gap in the fence, and disappeared into someone's backyard.

Janna took a deep breath and tightened her hold on the bag.

She turned and took a step.

The white car pulled into the alley. Engine roaring, wheels spitting gravel, it sped straight toward Janna.

For a split second, she froze. The car kept coming, faster and faster, its front grille like a shark's mouth.

No time to see who was driving. Whose foot pressed the gas pedal to the floor. Janna's blood began to flow again and she dived out of the way, landing hard against a backyard fence.

Brakes squealed. Brake lights flared red.

Janna was up, still clutching her bag, scrambling along the fence.

The engine whined.

He's backing up! Got to get out of here!

Gasping in panic, Janna ran along the fence,

found the gap the cat had gone through. It was a loose board. She shoved her shoulder into it, and it gave.

But not enough.

Desperately, she pushed her way into the narrow space. Felt something snag the shoulder of her T-shirt. Heard the engine roar.

He's coming again!

Janna shoved herself as hard as she could through the gap and fell onto her knees. Rolled away, scrambled up, tore across the yard and into the next one.

Wet sheets hanging from a clothesline wrapped around her. She twisted and turned, batted them away until she was free.

Kept running. Through a hedge, over a kid's bike, behind a toolshed. Her heart pounded, roared in her ears.

Through another yard, another hedge, and suddenly she was on the street she'd been trying to get to from the alley.

A quick glance, up and down.

No white car. No cars at all.

Janna dashed across the street, down another alley. Breath rasping in her throat. Feet pounding like her heart.

She burst out of the alley and into the road.

From her left, the roar of an engine.

No time to stop. Janna raced full out across the road and into a field that seemed to stretch for miles. Wildflowers and thick weeds covered its surface. Clumps of trees, rocks, some scattered garbage.

Behind her she heard the squeal of brakes, then the whine of the engine again. He was driving beside the field, waiting for another chance.

A chance to run her down.

Should have gone back! Should have run to one of the houses!

Too late now. Keep going. Keep going! Janna thought as she fought her way through the tangled weeds.

Desperate to get away, Janna veered into the middle of the field. Through a clump of willow trees, their drooping branches tangling in her hair. Splashed across a ditch, felt the muddy water spatter onto her bare legs.

Her chest ached now. Her breath whined in her throat like the engine of the car. Her feet burned inside her new sneakers.

Janna slowed a little, risked a glance over her shoulder.

She couldn't see the car anymore, but she knew it was out there, somewhere.

She turned and kept running. Her bag

bumped against her leg, dragged on her arm. She hitched the strap over her shoulder and across her chest. Kept moving, her head swiveling back and forth.

Then she saw the car. On her left now, moving along the road at the far end of the field.

Janna dropped to her knees. Looked to her right — too far to go back that way, to the safety of the houses.

Straight ahead was the road that would take her to the theater.

And lumbering down it, billowing exhaust, was a bus.

My only chance, Janna thought as she leaped up. Running all out, she tore though waist-high weeds and shot across the road, waving her arms.

The bus hissed to a stop. As Janna climbed on, she saw the white car flash by in a cloud of dust.

She never saw the driver.

Thank goodness for adrenaline, Janna thought as the curtain closed for the last time that night.

Without it, she would never have made it

through the performance. But by the time the bus let her off at the theater, she had only half an hour to get into makeup and costume. The pre-show jitters set in, the adrenaline started pumping again, and she danced even better than the night before.

Now, though, she was ready to collapse.

"Know anybody who could give us a lift back to the motel?" she asked Toni as they left the stage.

"Maybe Jake," Toni suggested.

"Good idea. Let's find him and ask." Janna glanced around the crowded wings, didn't see Jake.

She turned back toward the stage.

Ryan stood there, staring at her.

The moment their eyes met, he turned away.

Janna shivered. How long? she wondered. How long had Ryan been watching her?

For a minute?

Or for days?

"Jake was on the other side of the stage," Toni said, breaking into Janna's thoughts. "But he's got to stay and help repaint a flat. We'll have to hoof it."

Blinking away the memory of Ryan's eyes

on her, Janna followed Toni downstairs to the dressing room.

Liz wasn't there yet, thank goodness. The last thing she needed was a run-in with her.

As Janna removed her makeup, Gillian picked up one of Janna's muddy sneakers. "I can't believe he tried something again so soon. This guy's really over the edge."

"You *are* going to report it, aren't you?" Toni asked, stepping out of her yellow skirt.

"I guess so." Janna wiped the dark liner from her eyes and took off her own costume. "Of course, I didn't see the driver. Or the license or anything. Just a white car."

"No wonder. You were too busy running for your life," Gillian said. "Report it, Janna. At least the police'll know about it in case something else happens."

As she hung up her dress, Janna shuddered slightly at the thought of what else might happen.

Just be ready, she told herself. Be ready for anything.

"Are we going to the coffee shop?" Toni asked. "I'm starving."

"I am, too." Janna glanced at Toni and reached into her duffel bag for a clean pair of shorts. "But I'm . . ."

She gasped and yanked her hand out.

It was covered with blood. Blood that seeped between her fingers and dripped slowly down her wrist, bathing her bare arm in a glistening river of red.

Chapter 17

"What happened?" Toni cried, staring in horror at Janna's hand.

"I don't know!"

"Quick, wrap something around it!" Toni grabbed a towel off the back of her chair and tossed it to Janna.

"There has to be a first-aid kit somewhere!" Gillian said, rushing to the door.

"No, wait!" Janna said, gingerly wiping some of the blood away. "It's not . . . look, I'm not hurt! I knew I didn't feel anything. Besides, there's nothing sharp in my bag. Just some clothes and my wallet."

"Then where'd the blood come from?" Gillian asked, coming back inside.

"I don't know," Janna said again. She wiped some more of the blood off her hand, then hauled her bag onto the dressing table. She pulled it open wide and looked in.

Lying on top of a small pile of clothes was Bearyshnikov.

The bear's round little stomach was slit down the middle.

His stuffing had been torn out and was scattered around him.

In the cavity where the stuffing belonged was a pool of thick blood.

His pudgy legs were cut off. Drying blood crusted in the golden fur around the hacked-off stumps.

Beside the eviscerated body lay the little bear's head, bloody tears spilling from his brown glass eyes.

Janna's own eyes filled with tears.

She felt blindly behind her for the chair and dropped into it, sickened.

"Sick," Gillian declared, her face pale. "This is . . ." she shook her head. "I wonder where the blood came from."

"Please!" Toni groaned. "Don't even think about it."

"Who's doing these things?" Janna muttered, clenching her fists. The sick feeling was mixed with anger now. "Who hates me so much? Who *is* it?"

"And even worse," Gillian said grimly, "how did he get into our room?"

A burst of laughter came from down the hall. And then Liz entered the dressing room. Her smile started to fade as she glanced at Janna. When she noticed the bloodstained duffel bag, it completely disappeared.

"What happened?" she asked.

"Take a look," Gillian suggested.

Liz wrinkled her nose and peered into the bag. "Oh, gross!" she cried, jumping back. "Thanks for warning me!"

Her nose still wrinkled with distaste, Liz moved to the far end of the dressing table. "How'd that happen?" she asked, opening a jar of cold cream.

"Good question," Janna said. She pulled on the dirty T-shirt and shorts she'd been chased in earlier. "And don't even start talking about Ryan, Liz. I won't believe it."

"Okay, fine. Believe what you want." Liz shrugged as she smeared the cream on her face and grabbed a wad of tissues. "Too bad, Janna," she said. "I mean, that bear was your good-luck charm, right? I don't happen to be superstitious myself, but lots of actors are."

Janna zipped the bag closed.

"This guy I knew from last summer always recited a multiplication table before he went on," Liz continued. "If he could say it forward and backward without having to stop and think, he knew he'd have a good show." She turned to Janna and smiled. Her lips were very red next to the white cold cream. "Maybe you should try something like that. I'd hate to see your luck run out."

As she left the theater with Toni and Gillian, Janna took the bag with the mutilated bear in it and stuffed it in a trash can near the stage door.

"So long, Bearyshnikov," she murmured.

"You can get another one," Toni said, looking ready to cry. "Let's go shopping tomorrow."

"It wouldn't be the same." Janna felt naked without her bag. She stuffed her hands in the pockets of her shorts. She'd really miss the bear, but she couldn't rely on luck, for anything.

She had to rely on herself.

"Listen, I know this is going to sound weird after seeing all that blood, Janna," Toni said as they turned out of the graveled drive and onto the road. "But I'm still starving. If I don't get something to eat, I'll absolutely collapse."

"That's okay," Janna told her. "I'm actually hungry, too. Let's stop at the 7-Eleven and stock up on junk."

As they walked along, Janna kept glancing around, back and forth, over her shoulder.

The white car had come out of nowhere before. It could do it again.

They were coming up on the 7-Eleven when she saw him.

He was walking behind them, his pale blue shirt bobbing like a ghost in the darkness.

But the darkness wasn't total. The road had streetlights. And when he walked underneath one, Janna saw him clearly.

Following them. No. Following *her*.

Janna's heart speeded up. The adrenaline she thought was used up for the day kicked in again, stronger than ever.

"Don't look back," she murmured. "But we've got company. Don't look!" she repeated as Gillian and Toni started to turn around.

"Who is it?" Toni hissed.

"Stan."

Gillian sucked in her breath. "Are you sure?"

"Perfectly."

"What are we going to do?" Toni asked.

Janna smiled grimly. "We're going to get him."

Chapter 18

"Get him?" Toni repeated. "What are you talk- ing about? Janna, we can't just go chasing after him! I know how mad you are, but . . ."

"We're not going to chase him," Janna whis- pered. "We're going to trap him. We'll go into the 7-Eleven and call the police. Then we'll keep walking, like we don't even realize he's behind us."

As Janna spoke, she turned her head toward Toni. Caught a glimpse of Stan out of the cor- ner of her eye. Good. He was still following.

But not for much longer.

She'd be rid of him soon. He'd be out of her life.

Soon, Stan, she thought to herself. *Soon.*

As casually as they could, the three girls crossed the small parking lot of the strip mall and entered the 7-Eleven. Toni and Gillian stayed by the big glass window in front, Gillian pretending to flip through a magazine, Toni looking at bags of potato chips and popcorn.

Janna went to the back of the store, fed a quarter into the pay phone, and called the police. When she hung up, she hurried up front. "Is he still there?" she asked.

"He went into the video store next door," Gillian said. "We haven't seen him come out yet. I don't think he noticed us watching. I think he's just in there waiting for you."

"Are the police coming?" Toni asked.

Janna nodded. "Come on, let's get out of here. I told the police we'd be on the sidewalk. I have to point him out to them."

Toni paid for a bag of popcorn, and the three girls strolled back outside.

They were only a few feet down the sidewalk when Janna saw Stan again.

"He's still back there," she murmured. "He doesn't have a clue."

Janna forced herself to walk casually. To laugh at a joke no one had told. To make conversation about the performance.

But her hands were shaking, and her heart pounded with excitement.

She wasn't the hunted this time around.

She was the hunter.

"I think I see them!" Gillian whispered. "They're at the corner up ahead."

Janna narrowed her eyes. Gillian was right. A blue-and-white police car had pulled up at a stop sign. The driver glanced their way, then turned the wheel and headed toward them.

Suddenly Toni gasped. "Stan sees them, too! Janna, he's turned around!"

Janna spun around. Saw the pale blue of Stan's shirt as he passed under a streetlight. He walked at a normal pace. His hands were in his pockets, his head was up.

Like he just happened to be out for a late-night stroll, Janna thought angrily. She could almost hear him — "But officer, how could she think I was following her? You saw me — I was going in the opposite direction."

Going away from them.

Getting away.

No! Janna thought. She couldn't let him. Not now. Not when she was so close to getting him out of her life for good.

Furious, Janna broke away from Toni and Gillian and tore down the sidewalk after him.

She wouldn't let him get away, not after everything he'd done to her.

She had to stop him, now!

Stan didn't look back, but he was picking up

his pace a little, his arms swinging at his sides now.

Janna ran faster, her new sneakers pounding hard on the sidewalk.

The police car should be here by now! Where was it?

And then Stan glanced over his shoulder.

Janna saw his eyes widen. He stood stock-still for a split second, then turned and ran.

Janna tried to run faster. Tried to narrow the gap between them. But now that Stan was running, too, the gap began to widen again.

Desperate to stop him, Janna shouted his name. "Stan! Stop! Stan!"

Hearing her call his name seemed to stun him. For a split second, Stan slowed down.

It was all Janna needed. Putting on a last burst of energy, she closed the distance between them, reached out and shoved him from behind as hard as she could.

Caught off balance, Stan stumbled forward, then fell to his knees.

"You almost killed me!" Janna screamed, slamming Stan's back with her fists and forcing him to the sidewalk. "You hear me? You almost killed me, but now you're caught, Stan! You're trapped! How does it feel? Huh? How does it feel?"

Stan didn't even try to answer. He took Janna's raging blows without a word.

Behind her, Janna heard a single blip from the police siren. Tires crunched on gravel. Car doors slammed.

Two uniformed police officers raced over and pulled Janna away.

"He's the one!" Janna shouted. "He's the one who's been after me. He followed me all the way from Glenwood Junction!"

One of the officers grabbed Stan by the arms and lifted him to his feet. He slumped in the policeman's grasp. He didn't resist. He stared straight at Janna.

"You're sure he's the one who's been bothering you, miss?" the taller policeman asked.

Furious and breathing hard, Janna looked into Stan's eyes.

They were full of desire, gazing at her with admiration even now.

"I'm sure," Janna said between breaths. "He's the one. His name's Stan and he's been stalking me."

"Janna!" Stan whispered.

Janna ignored him. "He started back in Glenwood Junction," she said. "That's where he first saw me, in a theater. I'm a dancer, he was in the audience. I didn't even know him.

He's got some kind of . . . crush on me. And when I came up here, he came, too. He won't leave me alone."

The police officer turned to Stan. "You have anything to say about this?"

Stan licked his lips and murmured something.

"What?" the officer said. "Speak up."

Stan swallowed. He looked nervous, but his shining eyes never left Janna's face. "I love you," he said. "You have to understand. I love you."

"Love me?" Janna shook her head in disbelief. "You tried to kill me! When you couldn't drown me, you tried to run me over!"

Stan shook his head. He started to speak, but Janna cut him off.

"And my bear!" Janna continued angrily. "My stuffed bear. You stole it, Stan. And then you gave it back to me covered with blood! Is that what you do when you love somebody?"

The policeman cocked his head at Stan. "Doesn't sound like a crush," he remarked. "Sounds more like an obsession."

"That's exactly what it is," Janna agreed. "He's obsessed with me. He's been stalking me. And I want him stopped before *I'm* the one who winds up covered with blood!"

"Janna, I . . ." Stan stammered. "I . . . I didn't . . ."

The policeman interrupted. "We can talk about this downtown, Stan."

"But . . ." Stan shook his head as if he were trying to clear it. "But I didn't . . ."

"Come on, Stan," the police officer said. "Let's get out of here so this young woman can go home, okay?"

As he spoke, the officer moved over and took Stan by the elbow. He kept talking, his voice low but firm as he led him away from Janna toward the police car.

Janna watched, still shaking.

"Officer! Officer!" a voice called out from across the street.

Turning, Janna saw a brown-haired girl rush up to the police car.

"Carly!" Stan cried out.

"Shut up, Stan!" Carly interrupted. She grabbed the police officer's arm. "Please, you're making a mistake! Stan didn't do anything wrong."

"I'm sorry, miss, but we just need to take him to the station for a few questions." The officer helped Stan into the car.

"Please!" Carly pleaded.

Janna watched as the car pulled away.

Through the side window, she could see Stan's eyes, still watching her hungrily.

"This is a mistake!" Carly cried out as the car turned the corner.

"It's not," Janna said. "I'm sorry, but it's not."

Carly whirled around. "You!" she spat out. "This is your fault!"

"Are you crazy?" Gillian said. "Janna didn't do anything."

"Oh, sure!" Carly snapped. "The police just took Stan away. Whose fault is that?"

"Look, he followed me around," Janna said. "He tried to drown me. Run me over. You want my advice? Get him to a doctor."

"Thanks a lot," Carly sneered. "He was okay until you came along. I wish he'd never seen your face."

"So do I," Janna shot back, as Carly stomped off. "So do I."

"Have the police called you?" Gillian asked Janna the next night.

"Not yet," Janna told her. She sat down in one of the green room chairs and stretched her legs out. "I'll call them later, after the show."

"I wonder what happened with Stan," Toni

said, pouring herself a cup of coffee. "Do you think they arrested him?"

"I don't know," Janna said. "I guess I'll have to make a formal complaint or something. And I will, too. Anything to keep him away from me."

"He looked so totally pathetic," Toni remarked, sitting down on the lumpy couch. "I almost felt sorry for him."

"I know what you mean," Janna told her. "But just remember what he did." She glanced at the clock and stood up. "Anyway, it's over now," she added with a grin. "I can't believe how great it feels!"

Leaving Toni and Gillian in the green room, Janna walked quietly through the darkened wings toward the stairs. She had to change into her final costume.

As she trotted down the stairs, she thought again about how great she felt. Stan was out of her life now. She was free.

When she reached the bottom of the stairs, she saw Ryan standing in front of her dressing room. She stopped walking.

Ryan stayed where he was, and for a moment, the two of them stared at each other. Neither said a word.

Then Ryan's gaze slid away from Janna's face. He began walking toward her, but his beautiful, gold-flecked eyes were focused on the stairs behind her.

Janna didn't move.

Ryan brushed past her. She heard his footsteps going up the stairs. Fainter and fainter.

And then he was gone.

So cold, Janna thought with a shiver. He's been so cold ever since I told him to leave me alone.

What do you expect? she asked herself. And why are you complaining? It's what you wanted, isn't it?

Giving herself a mental shake, Janna continued down the hall and into the dressing room. She unzipped her blue-striped dress and stepped out of it. Flinging it over the back of a chair, she turned to the rack of costumes against the wall and pulled her pink and green dress from its hanger.

It slithered through her fingers and fell to the floor in a heap. A scrap of green, threads hanging from it, stayed in her hand.

Janna reached for the dress again and held it up in both hands.

The sleeves hung by threads. Long, ragged

strips hung from the neck to the waist, from the waist to below the hem.

The costume was torn to shreds as if a wild animal had clawed at it.

Pinned to one of the shreds was a note.

Next time, you'll be in it.

Chapter 19

"What do you mean, you let him go?" Janna cried into the telephone.

The police officer's voice stayed calm. "We had to, Miss Richards. As I explained, Stan March has no record of anything, not even a speeding ticket."

"You didn't see him chasing me around in that car yesterday," Janna said through clenched teeth.

"Well, that's another thing," the policeman told her. "Seems he doesn't drive a white car."

"So maybe he rented it!" Janna suggested angrily. "Look, you've heard about everything that's happened to me. Do you think I'm making it up?"

"No, ma'am, we don't think that at all." The officer paused a moment and Janna heard some papers being shuffled. "According to Stan

March, he did send you flowers and wrote to you. Plus he admitted calling you back in Glenwood Junction, and then writing a message on your mirror here in Braxton. But he says that's all he did."

"He's lying!" Janna cried. "I know I can't prove it, but he is!"

"I don't blame you for being upset," the policeman said. "He seemed a pretty strange character, but we can't arrest him for that. We *did* give him a warning, though. A very strong one. And one of the men gave him a nice escort out of town. Didn't get off his tail until he was halfway back to Glenwood Junction."

"Well, your warning didn't work," Janna snapped. "Somebody slashed one of my costumes tonight and left me a threatening note with it. And now that I know Stan March is still on the loose, I have a pretty good idea who did it!"

The policeman's voice became slightly more alert, and he promised they'd be on the lookout for Stan. "If he's back in town, we'll get him, Miss Richards."

Sure, Janna thought as she hung up.

She tapped her fingers on the phone and glanced around. She was in the theater manager's office, in the hall outside the wings.

She'd come here right after the last curtain, not even bothering to take off her makeup or change out of her costume.

She looked down at her blue-striped dress. It was from the first act. She'd thrown it on and raced onstage, forcing the stalker's latest threat out of her mind so she could dance. And she had — better than ever.

The slashed costume hadn't stopped her.

But Stan might.

The police had let him go. They'd escorted him halfway back to Glenwood Junction. He didn't drive a white car.

A white car.

Jimmy Dare's father had a white car, didn't he? Yes, and Jimmy borrowed it all the time, or he did when Janna was going out with him.

Why hadn't she thought of that before?

Quickly, Janna picked up the phone again and dialed Jimmy's home. While she waited for someone to answer, Toni stuck her head around the door.

"A bunch of us are going for pizza," she said. "You want to come?"

Janna nodded. "As soon as I'm through here," she said. "You'll never . . . hello?"

"Meet you there," Toni mouthed silently, and hurried off.

"Mr. Dare?" Janna said into the phone. "This is Janna. Janna Richards. Could I speak to Jimmy, please?"

"Jimmy?" Mr. Dare said. "Haven't seen him for a few days, Janna. He's got himself a job. About time, too." He chuckled.

Janna smiled. She'd always liked Jimmy's father. Too bad Jimmy didn't take after him. "Well, thanks, Mr. Dare."

"Anytime. Say, if you run into him, remind him that I expect a full tank when he gets back," Mr. Dare told her.

"Why would I run into him?" Janna asked. "I thought he was working."

"He is. He's driving all over the place, trying to sell encyclopedias." Jimmy's father laughed again. "And using my car to do it!"

Driving all over the place. Using his father's car.

His father's white car.

Standing in the theater office, Janna suddenly went cold.

Jimmy must have disguised his handwriting on the note, she thought. Just like he disguised his voice. When he realized he couldn't have me, he snapped. Now he wants to kill me.

As she reached for the phone to call the police again, she heard a loud click.

The hallway lights had gone off.

Go, she told herself. Get out of here now.

She sped out of the office and back to the wings. No one was around.

It was dark here, too, but not pitch-dark. A dim bulb glowed over the stage manager's table. The table was offstage right, just out of the audience's view. Beyond that were the stage doors, the quickest way out.

Janna was in the wings stage left. Keeping her eyes on that faint light, she headed through the wings toward the stage.

She'd almost reached it when she heard it.

A muffled noise.

Then a scraping sound.

Janna's mouth went dry. Her heart thundered.

The sounds had come from behind her.

Gripping the heavy folds of the open curtain, she glanced over her shoulder.

Ryan Mitchell stood there, a tire iron from the prop table clutched tightly in his hand.

Chapter 20

No, not Ryan! Janna thought. Not Ryan!

Janna's heart stalled, then started racing again as he took a step toward her.

"Don't!" she told him. "Ryan, please!"

He stopped, staring at her. "Janna, what's wrong? I want to talk to you."

Right, Janna thought. Just have a little chat with a tire iron in your hand.

"I can't talk now," she told him. "I don't want to talk now."

"I know that," Ryan said. He stayed where he was, about ten feet away from her. "You haven't talked to me for a long time, Janna, not since you saw me with Liz."

Janna's mind started racing along with her heart.

Not since you saw me with Liz, he'd said.

That's when all the real terror began.

After she'd told Ryan to leave her alone.

Stan might have stalked her. But he was harmless.

Ryan wasn't. Ryan Mitchell wanted to kill her.

"Janna," Ryan said. "Listen to me."

She shook her head. "I can't. I have to go." It was all she could think of to say. She could scream, but no one was around to hear her. "I really have to go, Ryan," she repeated. "Maybe we can talk tomorrow or . . ."

"I've waited too long already!" he burst out.

Janna stiffened, terrified.

"Okay, I won't talk," Ryan said. Quietly this time. "I'll ask you something instead." He cocked his head and smiled at her. "I left something for you in your dressing room. Did you find it?"

The image of her costume flashed across Janna's mind. Her pink-and-green plaid dress. Slashed and shredded to ribbons.

How could he smile? she wondered. How could he ask that with a smile on his face?

"I found it," she whispered.

His smile widened. Even across the shadowy wings, Janna could see the dimple at the side of his mouth. "What did you think?" he asked.

Janna started shaking. From anger. From fear.

Get out of here! she told herself. Stop trying to talk your way out. Stop trying to fool him.

Just get out of here, now!

Keeping her eyes on Ryan, Janna took a step backward. The heavy folds of the open curtain enveloped her. She gasped and tried to push them away.

Ryan was moving toward her.

"No!" she shouted, batting wildly at the thick folds of dusty red velvet. "Don't do this, Ryan! Don't do this!"

At last she found the edge of the curtain. Breaking free, she ran onto the stage.

"Janna, wait!" Ryan called.

Footsteps behind her. He was coming. Running fast. Getting close.

If he caught her, he'd kill her.

"Janna!" His voice was closer.

"No!" she screamed.

Her foot caught on something. The edge of a flat, a prop that hadn't been put away. She never knew what.

But she was stumbling. Trying to keep her balance. Trying to run, even as her arms shot out and her feet left the ground.

Her hands hit the stage. Her wrist bent awkwardly and pain shot up her arm. She tried to get her feet under her, tried to scramble up, but she fell to her stomach.

Behind her, footsteps again.

A rattling sound.

A dull thud.

A gasp.

Movement behind her.

Janna screamed and braced herself on her elbows. Got to her knees.

Screamed again as Ryan fell beside her. The tire iron skittered and clanged across the stage into the wings.

He tripped, too! she thought. You still have a chance!

She got her feet underneath her. Started to stand.

And then she noticed that Ryan wasn't moving. He was on his stomach, his arms flung out in front of him. His head was turned to one side. His eyes were closed.

A trickle of blood ran from the dark-blond hair at the back of his neck and dripped steadily onto the stage.

Janna was still staring at the blood when a voice whispered, "He only wanted to talk to you, Janna. Too bad you didn't listen."

Chapter 21

Slowly, Janna looked up.

Stan's girlfriend stood just beyond Ryan's feet.

Carly.

Janna swallowed, too frightened to speak.

Carly tucked a strand of soft brown hair behind her ear and smiled.

A deadly smile.

"Surprised?" she asked.

Janna just stared. Carly was dressed in black. Black jeans. Black, long-sleeved T-shirt. Black sneakers.

Like a shadow.

Keeping her eyes on Janna, Carly moved forward, skirting Ryan's body. As she walked, something rattled and clanged on the stage floor.

Janna's breath stopped when she saw what it was.

A two-foot length of heavy lead pipe with a thick chain attached to one end.

She held the pipe down, along the length of her leg, letting the chain drag behind her.

She stopped next to Ryan.

Letting her breath out, Janna glanced anxiously at Ryan. Carly had hit him with that pipe, hard enough to knock him out.

Hard enough to kill him?

"I don't think he's going to be able to help you, Janna," Carly said. She lifted her foot and nudged Ryan's arm with the toe of her black sneaker.

"Stop it!" Janna cried. She got all the way to her feet. She'd seen Ryan's back rise and fall. He was breathing. He wasn't dead. "Don't touch him again!"

Carly's eyes darkened. In one swift movement, she raised the pipe and cut the air with it.

The chain slammed across the boards, just missing Ryan's fingers.

Janna flinched and stumbled backward.

"Don't tell me what to do!" Carly was breathing hard. "Don't you ever tell me what to do!"

Janna steadied herself, but her gaze darted frantically around the stage and the auditorium. Carly was between her and the stage doors now. She couldn't go that way.

"Looking for a way out?" Carly asked. "Forget it."

Janna's throat was dry. It hurt when she swallowed. "I don't understand." She took another step back. "This is crazy. I don't understand why you're doing this!"

"Oh, very cute," Carly said sarcastically. She tapped the pipe against her thigh. "You're a lousy actress, Janna. You know exactly why I'm doing this."

"Stan," Janna murmured. "Stan was . . ."

"Stan was crazy about you!" Carly shouted. "I saw the way he looked at you, don't think I didn't!"

Janna shook her head. "But I . . ."

Carly slammed the chain against the stage again. "He thought he could hide it from me. But I knew something was up the minute he dragged me to that stupid show in Glenwood Junction. 'Wait'll you see the dancing, Carly!' he said. But I didn't watch the dancing. I watched *him*, Janna. And he never took his eyes off of you."

As Carly took a step forward, Janna backed

up. Took a quick glance over her shoulder. The stage left wings were behind her. A costume rack. The prop table. Beyond that, the door she'd come through from the hall.

She jumped, gasping, as the chain rattled again.

"You should have seen his face when he saw you at the club," Carly continued, slapping the pipe against her leg. "You *did* see it. Didn't he remind you of a dog, Janna? He did everything but drool. If he had a tail, it would have been wagging! I wanted to leave, but no! We had to say hello to you. And you opened your big mouth, Janna. You started asking questions about roses, and calling the theater. And that's when I knew!"

Janna inched backward, but she didn't dare look away again. Her eyes went back and forth between Carly's face and the pipe.

"I knew he was obsessed," Carly went on. "But with you, not with me! And it should have been with me!"

"Why didn't you talk to him?" Janna cried. "Why didn't you tell him to stop?"

"He left town before I even had a chance," Carly told her. "And you know where he went, don't you? He followed you here!" She narrowed her eyes. "Besides, it was too late for talk. He wouldn't have listened. He couldn't hear anything or see anything but you."

"So you came up here, too," Janna whispered, as she realized the truth. "You pushed the set on me. Called me from the phone booth. Tried to drown me in the pool. You were the one in the white car, and you . . ."

"Sliced up your bear and your costume," Carly finished. "You're catching on. It makes sense now, doesn't it?"

Janna just stared at her.

"I realized it didn't matter how far away you went," Carly said. "Stan would follow you. And even if he couldn't, he'd still be obsessed with you. You're like something hideous, growing inside Stan. And I have to cut you out!"

As she talked, Carly kept moving toward Janna, backing her into the darkened wings.

Gasping, Janna stepped backward.

Carly kept coming. She was holding the pipe up now, coming closer to Janna.

Janna took one quick glance over her shoulder. Saw the costume rack, black leather jackets hanging from it. The prop table. Wrenches. Another tire iron.

"Don't even think about it, Janna," Carly warned.

Janna whipped her head around.

"By the time you make it to that tire iron, this chain'll be wrapped around your neck. Imagine how that'll feel," Carly said with a grim smile.

Janna didn't say anything. She wasn't thinking of the prop table. She took another step backward, one hand behind her. Stretched her fingers out, feeling.

There!

Her fingers closed over a smooth metal tube.

Janna spun around. Leaped behind the costume rack. Grabbed hold of it with both hands and shoved the rack straight at Carly.

And then Janna was running. Behind her, she heard the wire hangers pinging loudly as the jackets fell from them.

She was on the stage now. Ryan's body stretched out in front of her, still not moving. She wanted to stop, but she couldn't. She couldn't help Ryan if she were dead. She had to get out — across the stage, through the wings and out the stage door.

She was just past Ryan's head when the heavy metal chain lashed out and whipped around her ankle.

Screaming in pain, Janna crashed to the stage floor.

Chapter 22

Carly yanked on the chain and Janna screamed again as it cut through her sock and sliced into her ankle.

"Missed your neck, didn't I?" Carly hissed. "Next time, I won't."

The chain came loose. Janna scrambled to her feet. Carly raised the pipe.

Suddenly Janna kicked out. Kicked like she'd been taught in hundreds of dance classes. Used the strong muscles in her leg, pointed her toes inside the black-and-white saddle shoe, and slammed her foot into Carly's chin.

Carly grunted and staggered back, but Janna didn't wait to see if she fell.

She was close to the front of the stage. Go that way! Straight up the aisle, through the lobby and out that way! Behind her, she heard the chain rattle. She didn't look back as she jumped down into the orchestra pit.

Janna staggered into a music stand and it fell with a crash. Another one blocked her way. She picked it up and threw it aside. Scrambled through a maze of chairs toward the narrow steps at the front of the pit.

She clambered up the steps, flipped over the railing. And then she was out, a river of red carpet stretching up the center aisle to the lobby doors.

She ran up the aisle, her ankle throbbing, slowing her down.

Gasping for breath, Janna finally reached the center doors and fell against one of the bars.

The door didn't open.

She shoved at the bar, then slammed her hands against the other one, pushing, trying to open the door.

"Your luck's running out," Carly called from behind her.

Janna whirled around.

Carly was moving up the center aisle. She walked slowly and steadily. Her eyes were narrowed to slits and glittered dangerously. Blood dripped from her chin.

Janna broke to her right, toward the far door.

It was locked, too.

"Two down, one to go," Carly called out. "There's another door this way, Janna. Want to try it?"

Pushing away from the door, Janna ran down the side aisle toward the stage.

When she reached the end of the aisle, Carly was waiting for her.

Swinging the pipe.

With a cry, Janna turned and headed back up the aisle.

Halfway up, another set of stairs, leading to the balcony.

Janna used the bannister to pull herself up the steps. Get up to the balcony, she thought. Cross to the other side. Down the steps, down the left aisle and up onto the stage.

She reached the balcony and started along the back, behind the seats.

Halfway across, Janna froze.

Carly was waiting for her on the other side of the balcony.

"You don't get it, do you?" Carly asked. "You're trapped, Janna. You can't get away."

"You're crazy!" Janna screamed. "You don't know what you're doing!"

"I know exactly what I'm doing," Carly said. "I'm cutting you out of Stan's mind. Out of his life."

"I don't want him!" Janna cried. "Don't *you* get it? I don't want Stan!"

"Shut up!" Carly raised the pipe and brought the chain crashing down on a seatback. "It doesn't matter what you want! It matters what *he* wants. And he wants you. But when you're not around anymore, he'll be mine again."

Carly lunged forward.

The chain whipped past Janna's head. She felt the air stir against her cheek and screamed.

The chain rattled as Carly swung the pipe back.

Janna staggered forward, bumped against the back wall of the balcony. And saw the four steep steps that led up to the lighting booth.

A phone! The booth had a telephone! She'd lock herself in, call for help.

She tore up the steps and crashed through the door into the glass-fronted booth.

Too late.

Carly was in the door, coming for her.

Janna pushed the chair at her, kept going, through the other door of the booth. Up some more steps, not even thinking where they led until she got there.

The catwalk.

She was on the catwalk that stretched from the middle to the back of the auditorium. The long, narrow metal plank hung from the ceiling by thick wires, swaying like a suspension bridge as Janna began to crawl along it.

She had no choice. She couldn't go back. If she had to, she'd jump. Jump before Carly pushed her.

When she was halfway out, the catwalk began to shake.

"Don't look down, Janna," Carly called out from behind her. "You might get dizzy and fall!"

Carly laughed and the catwalk shook.

Janna closed her eyes, clung tightly to the sides.

The chain rattled. The walk swayed dangerously. Janna glanced back.

Carly was standing on the catwalk, swinging the pipe. Coming closer.

Trapped, Janna thought. I'm trapped!

Keeping her eyes on Carly's face, Janna slowly rose to her feet. "Take your best shot, Carly!" she cried. Her heart raced and her knees shook, but her voice was steady. "Come on!"

Carly took another step forward on the narrow catwalk. The pipe hung from her hand. The chain dragged and clattered behind her.

Get ready, Janna told herself. Duck Carly's shot and then knock her down.

Breathing heavily, she waited for Carly to make her move.

Carly came a step closer, then stopped. Raising her arm, she began to swing the pipe above her head. The chain whirled around, faster and faster, whining through the air.

Janna split her concentration between Carly's mad eyes and the whirling chain.

Her muscles tensed.

Her teeth clenched.

Adrenaline flowed.

Carly put everything she had into her swing. The chain glittered in the dim light as it flew toward Janna's head.

Janna ducked.

She felt the chain brush across her hair. She started to rise, to make her own move.

Then Carly lost her balance on the swaying catwalk and toppled over the side.

Her scream echoed in the empty auditorium as she tumbled through the air.

When she hit the seats below, the screaming stopped.

Later, Janna stood at the stage doors with Ryan, watching the ambulance and police car drive off, sirens shrieking.

"I can't believe Carly's still alive," Janna said. She glanced at Ryan. He had a bandage on the back of his head, and his lean face was pale. But he was going to be all right. "I'm so glad you're okay," she told him.

Ryan smiled. "I've got a hard head, Janna. Like you." He put his arm around her and pulled her close. "At least you know now that I'd never hurt you."

Janna nodded. "I should have known before, I guess. I should never have suspected you, not even for a second. But you were acting so cold." She sighed. "I know, I know — I asked you to stay away from me."

Ryan squeezed her tight. "It wasn't easy for me, Janna."

Janna leaned against him, feeling safe. It was over now. Finally, it was over. "Anyway, when you said you'd left something for me in the dressing room, I thought it was my ripped-up costume." She glanced up at him. "What were you talking about?"

Ryan stepped back from her. "Don't move," he said. He disappeared into the backstage area. Janna heard his feet going down the stairs.

He was back a moment later. He hurried across the stage and handed her a white shoe box tied with a blue ribbon. "I guess you didn't see this before," he said with a smile that showed his dimple. "I heard all about what happened to . . . well, open it and see."

Janna untied the ribbon and pulled the lid off.

Lying on a bed of tissue paper was a stuffed bear with golden brown fur and eyes to match. A tag tied to its paw said, *For luck, with love. Ryan.*

Janna looked up into Ryan's gold-flecked eyes. Setting the box aside, she put her arms around his neck and kissed him.

"You think maybe we could start over?" Ryan whispered, his lips against hers.

"I think we already have," Janna whispered back, and kissed him again.

THRILLERS

D.E. Athkins
- ❏ MC45246-0 Mirror, Mirror $3.25
- ❏ MC45349-1 The Ripper $3.25

A. Bates
- ❏ MC45829-9 The Dead Game $3.25
- ❏ MC43291-5 Final Exam $3.25
- ❏ MC44582-0 Mother's Helper $3.25
- ❏ MC44238-4 Party Line $3.25

Caroline B. Cooney
- ❏ MC44316-X The Cheerleader $3.25
- ❏ MC41641-3 The Fire $3.25
- ❏ MC43806-9 The Fog $3.25
- ❏ MC45681-4 Freeze Tag $3.25
- ❏ MC45402-1 The Perfume $3.25
- ❏ MC44884-6 The Return of the Vampire $2.95
- ❏ MC41640-5 The Snow $3.99
- ❏ MC45680-6 The Stranger $3.50
- ❏ MC45682-2 The Vampire's Promise $3.50

Richie Tankersley Cusick
- ❏ MC43115-3 April Fools $3.25
- ❏ MC43203-6 The Lifeguard $3.25
- ❏ MC43114-5 Teacher's Pet $3.25
- ❏ MC44235-X Trick or Treat $3.50

Carol Ellis
- ❏ MC46411-6 Camp Fear $3.25
- ❏ MC44768-8 My Secret Admirer $3.25
- ❏ MC47101-5 Silent Witness $3.25
- ❏ MC46044-7 The Stepdaughter $3.25
- ❏ MC44916-8 The Window $3.25

Lael Littke
- ❏ MC44237-6 Prom Dress $3.50

Jane McFann
- ❏ MC46690-9 Be Mine $3.25

Christopher Pike
- ❏ MC43014-9 Slumber Party $3.50
- ❏ MC44256-2 Weekend $3.50

Edited by T. Pines
- ❏ MC45256-8 Thirteen $3.99

Sinclair Smith
- ❏ MC45063-8 The Waitress $3.50

Barbara Steiner
- ❏ MC46425-6 The Phantom $3.50

Robert Westall
- ❏ MC41693-6 Ghost Abbey $3.25
- ❏ MC43761-5 The Promise $3.25
- ❏ MC45176-6 Yaxley's Cat $3.25

Available wherever you buy books, or use this order form.